# Fatal Success

# Fatal Success

## Dr. Jean Norbert Augustin

## (D.D, DMM)

## NOVELLA

# DISCLAIMER

This is purely a work of fiction. The story originated solely from the author's imagination.

No resemblance or identification with names, incidents and people - deceased or living – is intended or inferred.

Should any resemblance with the above be found, it would be purely coincidental.

**To the Holy Spirit from whom comes all my inspiration.**

*"Therefore, if anyone is in Christ, he is a new creation. The old things have passed away. behold, all things have become new"*.

2 Corinthians 5:17 (WEB).

# TABLE OF CONTENTS

# PREFACE

I usually write non-fiction books and have published six so far.

However, having been a high school language teacher for fifty-two years, I have developed a great liking for stories. As I taught literature – both, French and English – my imagination has been greatly enriched through contact with so many illustrious authors.

Additionally, I have always had a sharp sense of observation. I have learned a lot through watching the human comedy and – alas, the human tragedy, as well – on the world stage.

"*Fatal Success*" is a baby born of the union between observation and imagination.

In its embryonic stage, it was just an idea. At birth, it was no more than a simple sentence. Then, in its infancy, it developed into a five-thousand-word short story.

Now it has developed into full adulthood, being twenty thousand plus words long.

Time to stand on its feet.

I hope you enjoy the read.


The Author.

# ACKNOWLEDGEMENT

My gratitude to Mr. Michael Paul Johnson, Editor-in-Chief of WEB (World English Bible) – from which all quotations of the bible are taken – unless otherwise stated.

My heartfelt thanks to Miss Rimsha Anwar of Fiverr, my dedicated cover designer.

# CHAPTER 1

## MEET THE RAMGHUNYS

On that typically cold Mauritian afternoon in July, Sunita Ramghuny was busy fixing dinner in her small kitchen. Wrapped in her red sari, she constantly moved in quick but silent steps from the wooden square table covered with a greasy plastic tablecloth which had, once, been pink but which had begun to fade. She moved from slicing vegetables to rinsing the bites under the tap. The water being icy cold, she briskly shook her fingers every time she took them away from the tap water.

The atmosphere inside, however, was warm and cozy. The petroleum stove was lit, giving a red flame that licked the large sooty cooking pot that lazily sat on it. Rice was boiling in the cooking pot. Each time Sunita lifted the lid to test whether the rice was done, a thick vapour invaded the kitchen. Shrouded in it, the woman brushed it aside and, when her face emerged from it, droplets of sweat popped up on her forehead.

She cast a quick worried glance at the clock surmounted with two large alarm bells standing out like a pair of ears. "Nearly five," she said to herself, "and Ramesh is not yet back."

Once a very plump and beautiful woman, Sunita was beginning to lose her beauty. Not only because she was ageing, but also because of the hard work she had to do at home. Years ago, it was that beauty - her clear complexion, her long jet black hair and her enigmatic smile - that had first attracted Balkissoon, her husband.

They had first met at the wedding of one of Balkissoon's cousins, Anjani. Years had passed, but she still remembered the very first words the handsome Balkissoon had whispered to her: "You very much look like Vimla Kapoor, the Bollywood actress."

Blushing, the shy young girl had softly answered with a smile: "Thank you for the compliment. But I definitely couldn't ever sing and dance like her."

When Balkissoon's parents had gone to the Beeharrys' to ask for their daughter's hand, the request was, at once, accepted. The Ramghunys and the Beeharrys belonged to the same caste – which made things easy. Had they been of different castes, that would have posed a big problem. The Beeharrys were very orthodox Hindus. Sunita's father was even a very active member sitting on the managing committee of the village temple. Marrying his daughter to a man of a different caste would have suscitated a lot of problems for him – expulsion from the temple's managing committee, ostracization by the larger family and criticism on the part of the village folk.

Fortunately, they had been able to get married. As both families were not very rich, the wedding was celebrated in the simplest manner. Only the closest relatives and friends were invited. But they incurred much criticism from those who had not been invited. "We can't do otherwise," Balkissoon's father, Soodesh, would say: "We must cut our cloak according to our cloth. We can't satisfy people and put ourselves in financial difficulty." Consequently, the wedding was held in the strictest Hindu tradition.

One year after their marriage, Sunita suffered a miscarriage. The trauma was such that she didn't want to go through another pregnancy. Balkissoon quite understood her situation. But, nevertheless, he very much wanted to have a son.

"I understand you, Sunit." That was the endearing name by which Balkissoon called his wife. Likewise, she affectionately called her husband "Kissoon".

"I understand you, but a son would bear and carry the family's name down the generations. We won't be here forever, Sunit, and we wouldn't want our family's name to die with us."

After much hesitation, Sunita had given in to her husband's desire. Not only did she accept because of the family's legacy: she wanted her husband to understand how much she loved him. For the love of Kissoon, she was prepared to consent to that sacrifice.

Three years after their marriage, a son was born to them. In return of her sacrifice, Kissoon granted his wife the privilege of naming the child. Sunita chose the name "Ramesh" in honour of a god she revered.

As he grew up, Ramesh became the pride of his parents. In school, he did very well. He was liked by his teachers because he was well-disciplined and hard working. He passed his Primary School Leaving Certificate with very good grades. Unfortunately, he didn't manage to secure a seat in a State-owned high school because of the tight competition. Indeed, there were only a few State colleges but thousands of students in the race for admission to those schools.

Education in the private sector was fee-paying. Although it wouldn't be easy for Kissoon to pay for Ramesh's secondary education, he was, nevertheless, prepared to make a sacrifice to give their son an opportunity to obtain his Cambridge School Certificate and – if possible – his Higher School Certificate. His great desire was to give his son a better future than what he had personally known.

Moving up in the secondary sector was fairly easy. The lad was now aged 18. He was in Grade 12 at Prince Edward's High School. He was a very bright student and had always topped the list – much to his parents' pleasure. In two years' time, he would finish his schooling and would be able to look for a job to help his parents with the family's expenditures.

Not only was Ramesh good academically: he did equally well in sports. During his school's sport meetings and inter-school athletic meetings, he invariably obtained medals and trophies. He particularly excelled in the 200-metre and 400-metre races as well as in shotput and javelin throw. All his medals, cups and trophies proudly adorned a large shelf in his modest room furnished only with a single bed, a small cupboard and a couple of metal chairs.

Suddenly, Sunita heard familiar footsteps on the stone slabs in the yard. On sunny days, the yard was dusty and on rainy days it became unpleasantly muddy. Balkissoon had found a few large slabs with which he made a footpath leading from the road to the house door.

Entering the kitchen, Ramesh kissed his mother on both cheeks.

"Where have you been, Ram?" his mother asked.

Taking a seat, Ramesh answered: "To the village library, Mum. Some research for my Sociology assignment."

Having been only three years in school, Sunita wasn't quite sure she understood that academic jargon. But it was enough for her to know that her dear son was studying hard for his forthcoming exams. He would soon sit for his Higher School Certificate which, she was quite certain, he would pass with flying colours.

"You must be thirsty, son," the affectionate mother said. "Shall I make you a hot cup of tea?"

"Please, do, Mum. And let me have a couple of slices of bread with butter and jam."

And the proud mother started brewing a cup of tea for her dear son. As she had her back turned, Ramesh noticed that his mother no longer was that slim lady he had known. Lately, she had begun suffering from pains in her legs. Maye because of being on her feet for long hours to attend to all the housework.

"She's ageing," mused Ramesh. "I have to get through those exams at the very first sitting and get a job fast."

Once the tea was served, Ramesh blew over it to cool it a little. Meanwhile, he enjoyed the slices of bread with butter and strawberry jam.

"Your dad also won't be long. He must be hungry. I had better get those pulses and that vegetable stew ready before he arrives."

And she hurried to the stove. She put a pan on the fire and poured a few drops of oil into it. Once the oil started to sizzle, she dropped into it a mixture of ground spices and finally added the vegetable slices.

Just then, Ramesh heard footsteps on the slabs. "That must be Dad, Mum," he said, looking towards the door.

Indeed, Kissoon appeared in the doorway. "Hmmm," he sniffed. "Smells good!"

Taking off his large-brimmed straw hat, Kissoon kissed his wife on both cheeks while, wiping his mouth with the back of his hand, Ramesh got up to hug his dad.

He had leased a plot of land to grow vegetables. Having spent a whole day working in his vegetable plantation, Kissoon smelt of sweat. But his wife and his son didn't mind. For them, it was a testimony of his dedication to his family's welfare through his hard work.

"Will you take your tea …?" Sunita asked.

"Oh no, Sunit. Not until I have got rid of all that filth about me."

And off he went to have a bath.

Sunita emptied his large raffia bag. In it, were his aluminium lunch container, his spoon, his empty water bottle and a few vegetables he had brought from the plantation.

"As soon as Dad has taken his bath, I'll go to take mine as well, Mum."

"Ok, son. In the meantime, I'll finish the cooking and both of you can come back to have a hot dinner."

# CHAPTER 2

## FAMILY DINNER

"Quick, Sunit," Kissoon said, taking a place at table, "let me taste that nice smelling curry you've been cooking. I'm hungry as a wolf."

"Me, too, Mum," joined in Ramesh. "The very smell of your cooking makes my mouth water."

"You, men, are always hungry," said jokingly the good-humoured housewife.

In less than no time, she had served them both. She also placed on the table a jug of water and a bottle of soft drink. Finally, she took her place at table, too, and sat facing the two males.

"Nice food, Sunit!" Kissoon said as he plunged into his mouth a big spoonful of food.

"Whatever Mum cooks is good. An angel must have taught her."

"Oh, Ram," Sunita said with a smile, "you always think highly of me. I'm grateful, son."

"That's true, Sunit. Ram's right. Your cooking's really angelic."

"I'm glad you like my cooking," Sunita said with gratitude. "If my two men are happy, I'm happy, too."

And the three went on enjoying their dinner. Outside, they could hear the wind blowing. A thin wintry rain had begun to fall, too. They were really grateful and relieved to be inside.

"How about you, son?" Kissoon asked, turning to Ramesh. "How are your studies going?"

"Fine, Dad. They're going on fine. This afternoon, itself, I went to the library to prepare an assignment."

"And your exams, when are they due?"

"Mid-October, Dad. Not much time left."

Sunita got up from her seat and removed the empty plates and glasses. She put them in the sink and came back to wipe the table cloth on which there were a few drops of water and a few grains of rice that had fallen from their spoons.

"Sit down a moment, Sunit," Kissoon said. "Take some rest, dear. You've been working really hard today."

"That's true, Mum. Sit down and relax. I'll wash the dishes in a moment."

"Oh no, Ram," protested Sunita, "you've got your studies to do, son. That's a priority. I'll wash the dishes and you go and do your school work."

Indeed, that evening, Ramesh had plenty of work to do. He had an important assignment in Sociology to hand over on the following day. The Maths teacher had given him no fewer than forty numbers on permutation and combination, and he had an exposé to prepare for his General Paper class. He would have to literally burn the midnight candle!

"And do you have an idea of what you plan to do after that, son?"

Some time ago, Kissoon had heard Ramesh tell his mother that he very much wanted to be a policeman one day. Ever since he was a child, he had had a great admiration for the police uniform. He dreamed of wearing it one day.

"Well, Dad, I'm going to apply for admission to the Police Force. I've always wanted that."

Down deep inside, Kissoon had always wished his son get a job in one of the ministries of the country. A white collar job would really suit him. Working in a government's office, wearing a suit and necktie, working on important files, helping his Minister solve problems and attend to people's needs ...

Such was the vegetable planter's dream for his son. But he had kept that dream to himself. He didn't want to impose it upon him.

As for Sunita, she was prepared to consent to whatever her son would decide. It was *his* future, *his* life and *his* welfare that mattered, after all.

"May I know, Ram, why precisely the Police Force?"

Kissoon's question was not meant to oppose or challenge his son's decision, but he sincerely wanted to know if he had solid and valid reasons for joining the Police Force.

Ramesh moved his chair closer to the table and rested both arms on it. Then he cleared his throat to get ready to answer his father.

"Well, Dad," he began, "first of all, that has always been my dream. The very first time I saw a policeman in uniform, I was impressed by its elegance. I would really be proud to wear it one. But, mind you, Dad, it's not just for the uniform. It would be silly and vain to join the Police Force just because of a question of uniform. There are many more serious reasons…"

"And what are they, son?" interrupted Kissoon.

Sunita also was curious to know her son's motivations. As a submissive woman, she listened attentively without interrupting the two men.

"To tell you frankly, Dad," said Ramesh, resuming his explanation, "I am profoundly concerned with the conditions prevailing in the country. The problem of law and order is, indeed, very serious. And, day after day, it's getting worse. Crimes, aggressions, thefts, burglaries, hold-ups are increasing at a very fast pace. And, what's worse, drug trafficking is gaining ground. Cocaine, heroin, cannabis and now synthetic drugs are ruining our youth. Even school children are being targeted by unscrupulous drug pushers. Our country used to be a peaceful place where people lived in harmony. It was not without reason that we were called *"The Key and Star of the Indian Ocean"* and tourists used to call our country *"Paradise Island"*. But now tourists are robbed in public and their bungalows are broken into. Don't you remember, Dad, that Irish lady who was murdered in a five-star hotel in the West? Yet, there were security guards on the premises. And what was worse was that the couple was here for their honeymoon!"

Listening attentively, Kissoon acquiesced. "I remember that cruel and brutal murder, son. The whole country was shocked by that. Such a young and beautiful lady ..."

For the first time, Sunita joined in the conversation. Her female sensitivity was touched by the remembrance of that tragedy.

"What a pity!" she exclaimed, wiping her tearful eyes with a border of her sari. "Coming from so far to be murdered here during her honeymoon!" And she sniffed.

"And, after so many years," Ramesh resumed, "nobody has been arrested and jailed for that ruthless crime. Sure, two suspects were initially arrested and jailed. But they were soon released for some miscarriage of justice. And that's not the only unresolved case, Dad. Remember the young university student who was raped and murdered one evening only a few metres from her place ..."

"Oh yes," Kissoon broke in, lifting his hand and pointing a finger towards the East. "Yes, that was in the coastal village of Green Grove. The young girl had hardly alighted the bus and was about to reach home when she was attacked by a rapist. Her dead body was found on the next day in a bush nearby."

Unable to hear so much cruelty – brutality, in fact – against the womankind, Sunita sobbed and sniffed.

But Ramesh was determined to make his point and justify his decision.

"And not later than two weeks ago, an eleven-year-old Indian tourist girl was raped by the boat skipper who had taken a group of tourists to "*Seashell Island*" off the Southern coast … Tourists will no longer want to come to our country if that is not put an end to …"

Sunita sobbed and sniffed even louder. Kissoon shook his head to acquiesce. Ramesh knew he had given his parents enough good reasons to support his choice.

"But," resumed Kissoon, "how do you expect to change that if you join the Police Force? It's those at the top who can and make laws and take decisions to end that …"

"You're right, Dad. I'll be only a simple police constable at first. But I don't expect to remain a constable throughout my career. I'll keep on studying, take exams, apply for promotion and try to rise in the hierarchy … I'll study Law and master all the standing orders and relevant protocol …"

Father and mother felt proud, hearing their son using such eloquent and high-sounding words: hierarchy … standing orders … protocol …. They didn't quite understand everything. But, since these words were coming from their high-schooled son, they had to be good words and mean something important.

"Of course," Ramesh continued, "to be able to make significant changes in the Force, one needs to reach the top as Commissioner of Police. I don't mean to be overly ambitious, Dad. I'll have to move up one rung of the ladder at a time – one step at a time, if you will. But it won't be easy to get to the top. It will take hard work, it will demand time and I'll need to have luck on my side."

"If you're really motivated and determined, son, you'll be able to succeed. God will help you succeed."

"Your dad is right, Ram. Just believe in him and do your share."

Saying that, Sunita put her hands together as a sign of reverence, her face turned towards the picture of a Hindu god hanging on the wall. The picture must have been there for a long time. The colours had considerably faded and the glass frame was all greasy from the steam in the kitchen.

"And then, son," Kissoon said, switching the conversation to another subject, "you'll have to think also of your personal future. You won't spend the rest of your life staying single, running after robbers and tracking traffickers, will you? I hope not."

Interested by that pleasant turn in the conversation, Sunita pulled her chair a little closer.

"Your dad is right, Ram. You just cannot spend your life chasing criminals and let life pass you by."

The idea of love and marriage brought a smile to the young man's face. He had watched a number of Bollywood movies and had seen depicted in them perfect and even idealistic love affairs. True, many of them brought tears to the eyes. But, in the end, they all ended with beautiful and pompous marriages in fairy table style.

Physically, Ramesh didn't look bad at all. He never went unnoticed at family weddings. On his way back home in the afternoons, he often noticed college girls eyeing him or turning back to look at him.

His mother secretly already had a prospect for him. She had a distant cousin who had a beautiful daughter called Sweety. For Sunita, she would be a very good match for her son. However, she had never mentioned her secret wish to him, knowing that it was a bit early for that. And, more importantly, she wanted him to get through his exams at all costs.

Her son should not spend his life in a vegetable plantation like his father. Not that she despised that activity. Far from that: it had been their only source of income and was paying for their son's education. But it was too tiresome and too demanding. If he became a policeman, that would serve several purposes: realize his dream, help the family financially, give him a higher status in society and help him found a family.

But there was yet another important reason why her son's success mattered. Yes, he really had to pass his exams, join the Police Force and quickly rise in rank.

His family would, thus, be justified!

# CHAPTER 3

## UNPLEASANT VISITORS

Balkissoon had a younger brother called Gopal. He was a school Headmaster. His wife, Leela, was a secretary at the Ministry of Labour. Their daughter, Veena, was studying at Princess Alexandra University. She was doing her Master's in Psychology. Their younger son, Avinash, was studying at Royal College.

They had a large luxurious house in uptown Quatre-Bornes. They even had a bungalow on the Eastern coast where they spent most of their weekends, the winter and the end of year holidays. Recently, Gopal had sold his old Toyota and ought a brand new Mercedes.

It was true that Gopal's family was well off because of the posts the husband and the wife held. But, Balkissoon believed that there was another explanation for their relative opulence. He suspected Gopal had won a considerable prize in the National Lottery. One or two persons had mentioned that to Balkissoon. But that left the vegetable planter insensitive.

"If that's true," he would reply, "that's his good fortune. He's got his fate, I've got mine. Every human being has his own karma."

For him, his fate was found in his vegetable plantation. He would have to toil as long as God would give him life.

Because of their newly acquired social status, Gopal's family no longer frequented Balkisoon's family. Only when there was an urgency would they hypocritically inform or drop by. But that was once in a blue moon.

If Balkissoon was insensitive to his brother's family's attitude towards them, Sunita, on the other hand, felt the hurt. As their father had passed away when they were still very young, Balkissoon, who was the eldest child of the family, had started working at a very young age to help his younger siblings. He had financially helped Gopal when he was still studying. He bought his books and paid for his private tuitions.

Later on, Balkissoon again helped him with his wedding. A Hindu wedding, indeed, involves huge expenses. The ceremony lasts from Friday to Monday. The clothing and the food, especially, take the lion's share of the expenses. Thanks to his work in his plantation, Balkissoon had been able to finance to a large degree his younger brother's wedding.

And now, Gopal had forgotten all the good Balkissoon had done for him. All because of his new social position. Sunita had heard people say that money was the root of all evils, but had never paid much attention to that. Now, she had, in Gopal, a good illustration of that saying.

Nor was Gopal the only ungrateful member of his family. His wife, Leela, was, perhaps, worse. because of her post in government's service, she was always smartly dressed in beautiful and costly saris. She no longer spoke creole or Bhojpuri, the two languages she had been brought up in: she now spoke

French – *"la langue de Molière"*[1] (Molière's language)! Consequently, the whole family had followed suit.

Their daughter Veena also kept at a distance – especially since she had been enrolled at Princess Alexandra University. When she was still in high school, she sometimes came to see Ramesh. And, together, they would spend hours talking about school, studies and movies they had watched. But, as soon as she got into university, she had stopped coming to Balkissoon's place.

Sunita remembered the last time Gopal and Leela had dropped in at their place. It was a Saturday in April. Leela wore a beautiful blue sari and high-heel shoes. Large ear bangles hung on both cheeks, dangling each time she turned to left and right – which, Sunita thought, she did all too often.

---

[1] Famous French playwright (1622-1673). True name: Jean-Baptiste Poquelin.

When they arrived, Sunita was baking "*chapatis.*"[2] To accompany the *chapatis*, she had prepared a good spicy vegetable curry, a corned mutton salad and mango pickles. Balkissoon loved that. Whenever his wife made "*chapatis*", he would eat seven or eight – although they are considerably heavy on the stomach. And, on the next day, he invariably took about the same number for his lunch on the plantation.

While she was busy in the kitchen, Veena and Gopal were talking with Ramesh in his room. Balkissoon had gone to the shop to buy a bottle of soft drink to accompany their meal.

At a certain moment, Sunita overheard bits of what they were talking about. She took off the fire the thick iron plate on which she was baking the "*chapatis*", drew closer to the wall and stretched her ear.

She could hear the words "exams .... leave ... work ... your father ...."

---

[2] Flat and thin Indian bread baked on a griddle.

30

Understanding they were talking about education, Sunita listened more intently.

"Why don't you leave, Ramesh?" Leela was heard to be saying. "Your father's getting old …"

"Why should I, aunty?" answered Ramesh.

"Your dad's getting old. He can't finish his life working alone in his vegetable field. He needs help."

"I can't leave," Ramesh said, "when I'm just about to finish."

"With your help, Ramesh," broke in Gopal's voice "your dad can increase his production and you can …"

That conversation angered Sunita. She very much wanted to rush into the room and burst in anger. But, not being quarrelsome, she didn't want to start a brawl. Also she didn't want her husband to reproach her for having caused a dispute with *his* brother and sister-in-law. Had they been on *her* side of the family, she wouldn't have hesitated.

Just then, Balkissoon came back from the shop. "Are those *"chapatis"* ready, Sunit? I'm ready for five or six of them," he said heartily.

Sunita popped her head inside Ramesh's room, "Lunch is ready," she said. "Come and eat."

"Oh, already half past twelve," Leela said, casting a quick glance at her watch. We'd better leave, Gopal. We have to pick Veena at the beauty salon and Avinash at his gym and take them to lunch at *"Exquisite Exotic Cuisine"* restaurant."

The conceit in her tone was deafening!

Saying this, the couple left without kissing goodbye and hastened to their black Mercedes. Leela got into the driver's seat, Gopal slipped into the passenger seat and they drove off.

Sunita couldn't bear her sister-in-law's vanity. She couldn't understand how people of low origin could forget whence they come and become so vain once they have obtained a certain status.

After those unpleasant visitors' departure, husband, wife and son sat silently at the kitchen table to enjoy their modest lunch. They each had two dishes before them: one to hold the "*chapatis*", the other for the curry, salad and pickles. They ate, using their bare hands. Holding a "*chapati*" in one hand, with the other, they tore a small piece from it, picked a little curry with the piece and pushed it into their mouth. Every now and then, they licked their fingers or the back of their hand to pick a little curry that had slipped.

"Nice food, Sunit," Balkissoon said as he picked up his sixth "*chapati*".

"Indeed, Mum. This vegetable curry goes down very well with the pickles."

Sunita, meanwhile, had a burning question at the tip of her tongue. She hesitated a long while for fear of disturbing their peace or causing her husband's anger. But, finally, she spoke out:

"What was Leela telling you in your room?" she said, turning to Ramesh.

"Asking me to leave school," answered the young man between two bites.

Balkissoon started and stopped eating.

"What's wrong with her?" he said, visibly angry. "What does she have to do with your schooling?"

"Oh, Dad, she wants me to help you in the plantation instead."

"That woman's insane!" Balkissoon burst. "What's her problem if you're studying? *I* pay for your studies – not *she*! She's never given you the least cent!"

"She says you're getting old, Dad …"

"And so is she, isn't she?" said Balkissoon, mad with anger. "Everybody's getting old! And, anyway, why should she care about my age or my health? That's none of her business!"

Sunita felt she had to calm her husband's temper.

"Forget her, Kissoon," she said in a low tone. "That's jealousy on her part. Now that her children have succeeded in their studies and they've reached a certain level in society, they don't want you to succeed, Ram. For them, all our generation should be born and die as vegetable growers."

"Tomorrow," Balkissoon said, "I'll go and talk to her. I'll tell her ..."

"Oh no, Kissoon," pleaded Sunita, "please, no. Leave her alone. Just ignore her. Enough for us to know what kind of a woman she is. And what we choose to do is none of her concern. Please, finish your lunch, Kissoon."

"Mum's right, Dad," Ramesh said to further pacify his father. "Just forget her. I'll continue with my studies and work even harder to prove her wrong. Let's, for the present, enjoy our lunch."

Getting up from her chair, Sunita drew near, dumped a couple of "*chapatis*" into their dishes and added a large spoonful of curry to the little that was left.

===================================

That night, on his way to the bathroom, Balkissoon saw light filtering from under the door of Ramesh's room.

"The lad's still working," he said to himself.

Back in his room, he cast a quick glance at the clock:

1:50 am!

# CHAPTER 4

## TRAGEDY STRIKES!

The morning following that conversation, **B**alkisoon got up at 4:30 as usual. Sunita warmed up some rice, a few "*chapatis*" and some curry which she put in a raffia bag with a bottle of hot tea. She also added some rice lest Balkissoon should want something more and different. That was her husband's lunch.

Indeed, that day, Balkissoon had planned to spray herbicide and pesticide in his plantation. Indeed, his field was being invaded by weeds and creepers and infested with pests. If left untended, his crop might be completely ruined. He knew a Hindi version of the proverb that says: "A stitch in time saves nine".

So, after a quick breakfast of bread with butter and tea, he took his lunch bag, said goodbye to Sunita and off he went. He didn't want to awaken Ramesh for he knew his son had studied till late through the night.

He wanted to arrive at the plantation before the sun was high in the sky. With the sprayer strapped to his body, he would find it hard to labour under the scorching sun. To go to the plantation about three kilometres away, he daily rode his rusty Humber bicycle. It was a hard ride, indeed. In the morning, it was fairly easy going. But, after work, tired as he was, he had to cycle uphill. Having done that for the last twenty years, he was beginning to find it harder and harder. Age also was beginning to wear and weaken him. But that was the price he accepted to pay for his dear son's success and future.

Many a time, Sunita had volunteered to accompany him to the plantation to give him a helping hand. But he had adamantly refused: for him, it was the husband's exclusive duty to work and upkeep his family. For him, it was incumbent solely upon him as the husband to be the family's bread-winner. Work outside was for the husband; work inside was for the wife. Besides, he didn't want his dear wife to lose her youthful beauty, working in a vegetable plantation in sun and rain. Sunita's frequent solicitations had invariably collided with Balkisoon's adamant stubbornness. Finally, vanquished, the pleading woman quit asking.

No sooner had Balkisoon arrived at the plantation than he set himself to work. On that July morning, the wind was blowing rather violently. In a sense, it was refreshing, thus making the planter's work rather pleasant. But little did he know the consequences that that was going to have on him.

Indeed, in his haste to get the work done, he had forgotten to take the mask he used whenever he had spraying job to do. When he realized he had forgotten to take his mask, it was too late. No question of cycling back home to get it! The ride was far too tough. In addition to that, going back to get the mask would retard his work. He badly needed to get the job done so that his crop would be ready on time.

Indeed, he had a contract with a couple of hotels for the supply of vegetables. Soon the holiday season would come, tourists would flock to the country, the hotels would be crammed and huge amounts of vegetables would be needed. Of course, he was not the only supplier. In fact, he was only a relatively small supplier. But his carrots, cabbages and cauliflowers were about the best in the region.

Balkissoon observed that his vegetables were growing fairly well. After the spraying, however, they would look much better and he could expect to reap a good crop.

As he sprayed the plantation, he felt the weight of the can of herbicide on his back. The straps bit into the skin of his shoulders. As the wind blew, he felt refreshed. However, it brought the droplets of herbicide right back into his face. As he always had a thick towel which he used to wipe his hands with, he muffled himself with it. But this hampered his breathing.

At about twelve, he stopped to have lunch in the little wooden cabin where he kept his implements. After lunch, he rested for about half an hour. Then he resumed work to complete the spraying. When he left the plantation, the village church clock was striking three.

On his way back, he partly rode his rusting bicycle and partly alighted to push. Cycling uphill was much tougher that day.

"That road is going to kill me some day," he reflected.

That evening, when Balkissoon arrived home, he was unusually tired. After a quick bath, he went straight to bed. At dinner time, when Sunita went to call him to have dinner, she found him lying prostrated in his bed.

"Oh, Kissoon, Kissoon!" she screamed, "What's happened to you? Ram, come quick!"

When the young man heard his mother's screams, he threw away his books and rushed to see what the matter was.

"Hurry, son," Sunita cried, "quickly call a doctor!"

They had no telephone. That was during the pre-mobile phone era. Fortunately, they had a neighbour who had a fixed phone. Ramesh rushed to his place and begged him to call a doctor for him.

When the doctor arrived, he held Balkisoon's wrist, pressed a finger on the side of his neck, shook his head and declared the poor man dead. The death certificate he delivered read: "Cause of death: heart-attack due to stress and heavy chemical poisoning".

When she heard that, Sunita knew that Leela was no stranger to her husband's stress.

The poor woman felt lifeless. Throwing herself upon her husband's dead body, she wept her eyes out. Dishevelled and her sari almost undone, showing part of her back, she sobbed and wept and wailed.

"Oh, Kissoon, Kissoon," she sobbed, "why have you left me alone? What am I going to do with my life now? Oh, Kissoon, Kissoon, open your eyes, please …Talk to me just one more time …Tell me …"

And her voice got lost amidst her asphyxiating sobs.

Ramesh, with tears in his eyes, drew near and pulled his mother away. The poor woman abandoned herself in the arms of the young man who walked her away.

The vigil was held under a tarpaulin tent erected in their yard. Many neighbours came and so did relatives from various villages. They all – especially the womenfolk – wept with Sunita, hugged her and expressed their condolences.

Gopal and Leela came, too. But they stood at a distance, cast a quick glance at the corpse and left.

On the next day, a pundit, dressed in an ample white dhoti, came. He burned incense in a copper receptacle. Holding the censer by a chain, he swung it rhythmically, chanting prayers in Hindi. A thick smoke having an acrid smell rose and filled the atmosphere inside the marquee.

When the body was taken away to the cremation site, Sunita swooned. The womenfolk, out of solidarity, took her inside the house, poured fresh water over her face, fanned her and placed perfume under her nose to make her come to.

Ramesh, according to a Hindu tradition, had to go to the cremation ground to perform a ritual. After the pundit had read scriptures from a sacred book, he chanted prayers to which the attendees responded by a word that sounded something like "*swa-ha*". Those present threw petals of yellow flowers towards the pyre where the corpse lay under a pile of wood.

Then, they presented a firebrand to Ramesh. Dressed in white, the young man knew what he had to do. It was his duty as only son. Stoically, he walked to the pyre, bent down and set fire to the pyre. The fire was slow to start. A thick smoke rose, enveloping the corpse. Then red flames rose, licking the

logs. Crackling noises were heard as the flames grew larger. Soon the upper logs collapsed as the lower ones burned and turned to charcoal.

Suddenly, a loud crack was heard: Balkissoon's skull had burst!

Thus died that brave man, victim of his dedication to his work and loyalty to his family. His infallible sense of duty had taken its toll.

# CHAPTER 5

## SUNITA'S NEW ACTIVITY

After her husand's death, Sunita found herself in a very dire situation. As mother and son had had to observe a forty-day mourning and hold regular prayer sessions, the vegetable plantation had been neglected. The crop had been ruined. Without water, the vegetables had withered and turned brown. Weeds had begun to creep in anew. Carrots, cabbages and cauliflowers had rotted and lay dead in the field. Weeds had invaded the plantation. Worms, pests and maggots feasted on the fetid vegetables. It looked like the plantation also had been mourning Balkissoon's death.

As the contract could not be honoured, the hotels terminated it. Sunita had to take over the plantation work and try to sell whatever vegetable she could salvage to retailers at the market. But, as a woman, she couldn't do the same amount of work as her husband had been doing. Nor did she have the financial means and elementary "managerial" skills required to hire and manage helpers. She was only a poor illiterate widow with a student son and herself to feed.

Understanding his mother's situation, Ramesh volunteered to leave school and take charge of the plantation. With the money obtained from the sale of his vegetables, he could pursue his studies by taking private tuitions.

But his mother was adamant: "Not at all, Ram! You can't quit. Not when you are just about to finish your schooling. I don't want to hear you say that again."

"But, Mum …."

"Stop!" said forcefully Sunita, briskly moving her hand from side to side to express her disagreement. "Your father won't be happy. His *"atma"*[3] won't rest in peace, son. Understand that".

Mention of his dear father's soul not finding peace dissuaded the young man from his intention. An image flashed in his mind: he imagined his late father's soul roaming all over the country, looking for another body to reincarnate and find peace. That was a prospect he couldn't accept.

That thought convinced him that he should do as his mother said. He would work even harder at his studies and help his mother during weekends.

Sunita gathered the vegetables that were miserably left in the plantation and sold them to merchants at the market. When none was left, she made an arrangement with other planters: she would buy vegetables from them on credit and pay them after having sold the vegetables.

---

[3] In Hindi language: soul.

As there was a retail shop a few metres from her place, she asked for permission from the shopkeeper to place a table on the shop's verandah so that she could sell her vegetables to passers-y and inhabitants of the locality.

Not far away, there was textile factory. When the day's shift ended, many housewives, on their way home, would rush to her to buy vegetables to fix their dinner.

On Sundays, she had a different custom. St. Stephen's Roman Catholic Church was situated nearby. Masses were held hourly from eight to eleven. After each Mass, she made very good sales to the church goers. They would always find something to buy from her.

As time passed, Sunita got another idea. She began to make Indian cakes fried in boiling oil – like *"chilly bites"*[4] and *"samosas"*[5]. These are real delicacies in Mauritius, especially when eaten very hot! During lunch time and after their shift, the factory workers

---

[4] Small balls of crushed dholl mixed with spices and chilly.

[5] Triangular-shaped flour batter with potato curry filling.

came to buy her cakes. Eaten with bread, these made a quick and cheap meal.

That brought the widow an additional income. Meanwhile, Ramesh pursued his studies, many a night burning the midnight candle. Whenever he arrived home early, he joined his mother to help her sell her Indian fries and vegetables.

During weekends, he stood at their little "stall" at the shop to take care of the sales. Sunita would bake the fries and take them to Ramesh at various intervals, thus making sure there always was a regular supply to satisfy their buyers.

After some time, Sunita obtained yet another source of income. As their "stall" stood at a strategic site, a daily newspaper editor offered to give them a number of copies to sell. Of course, they accepted. In return, they earned a fair commission per sale.

That went on for some time. Their little business was bringing them enough money for their basic needs. They had enough food on the table, they could pay their water and electricity bills and Ramesh could buy whatever he needed for his studies.

However, one night as mother and son sat at the greasy table in the kitchen, Sunita noticed that her son was in a deep pensive mood. Worried, she asked: "What's troubling you, son? Why are you so sad and silent?"

Lately, Ramesh had noticed that his mother was really exhausted in the evenings. Sometimes, she would prepare dinner, serve her son and go to bed without dining. Her gait also had become slower. Sometimes, in the middle of her cooking, she would stop, sit on a chair and massage her legs. Standing long hours selling vegetables, cakes and newspapers at her stall was beginning to bear upon her legs. In the mornings, she also had to get up early to start baking her Indian fries. Lack of sleep was not making things any better.

"I'm wondering, Mum," the lad answered, "whether it wouldn't be better for me to leave school definitely and take over our little commerce. Thus, you could stay at home and take some rest."

"Absolutely not!" Sunita retorted, emphasizing the "*not*". "You absolutely have to get through your exams and join the Police Force. That's your dream, son. It's been your most cherished dream ever since you were a child. Besides, it would bring honour to your late father – wherever he may be."

Saying this, she lifted her head and looked heavenward.

"Mum, I see you are getting back home exhausted every evening. I don't mean to offend you. But you must realize you are no longer very young! If I give up my studies, I can take care of our little business."

After a few minutes of silence, he added: "I can even go back to the hotels and try to renegotiate a contract. If they accept, I can lease another plot of land, hire a couple of helpers and start a new plantation. The sale of our own vegetables will definitely bring us a better income."

As she listened to her son, Sunita was moved to tears. She stretched out her hands and held her son's.

"I am profoundly touched by what you say, son. But I insist on your getting through your exams. You must absolutely become a police officer to realize your dream and secure your future. You will eventually have to get married and raise a family. This vegetable business cannot afford you a safe future. There is a lot of competition in this sector and the climate is so unpredictable."

Seeing that Ramesh was in deep thought and looking anxious, she added jokingly: "Anyway, such a handsome boy like you shouldn't work in a vegetable plantation. Your place is definitely not there! You're made to wear that smart blue police uniform."

"You're right in a sense, Mum. But my concern is your health. I wouldn't want you to end your life the way Dad ended his."

Reference to her late husband brought tears to the poor woman's eyes. With the hem of her sari, she wiped her eyes which had turned red. Her mind rushed back to the conjugal bed where she had seen her husband's dead body lying prostrate across the bed. She saw his right hand pressing his breast. She realized he must have experienced a really excruciating pain before dying.

"If you become a police officer," she said, sniffing, "you will be able to rise in rank and become Sergeant, Inspector, Superintendent and – perhaps one day, Commissioner … Why not?"

"Please, Mummy, don't exaggerate. Me, Commissioner of Police? Don't joke."

"Why not, son? I know you are intelligent enough to rise as high as you will wish. Remember how many times you've ranked first in class."

Indeed, Ramesh was a very bright student. He had often come out first and received prizes from His Principal. Not only did he do well in academics, but he was also an excellent athlete. The shelf in his room was proudly adorned with numerous cups, medals and trophies obtained in javelin throw, in 200-metre and 400-metre races at inter-college sport events.

Ramesh realized that his mother was not wrong after all. He had not been used to working in the plantations. That work would never give him a good future, nor grant him security. As his mother had said, sooner or later, he would have to find a marriage partner and raise a family. Even if he should start growing vegetables, he wouldn't like his children to continue in the same field of activity. Also, the Mauritian climate was very uncertain and capricious. In summer, cyclones were very common; in winter, anticyclones made life very difficult. Those conditions severely damaged crops, thus causing great losses to planters.

Finally, after much thought, the young man made up his mind: he would follow his mother's advice and realize his father's dream by doing his best to join the respectable Police Force.

So he set himself to work arduously in order to obtain his Higher School Certificate – the passport to join the Police Department. With goodwill, hard work and strict discipline, he would be able to climb up the ladder and reach the highest rung possible in the hierarchy.

He remembered what his General Paper teacher used to tell the pupils to motivate them: *"Where there is a will, there is a way"*.

He resolved to follow that wise advice.

# CHAPTER 6

## RAMESH'S SUCCESS

At the end of the academic year, Ramesh sat for his Cambridge Higher School Certificate (HSC). He was perfectly confident he would get through. He had well prepared himself and the papers were not as difficult as he had feared they would be. There was only a number in Maths that was a bit tricky. But, after much struggle, he had managed to get over the difficulty.

He passed in all five subjects – three at main level and two at subsidiary level, as required by the University of Cambridge for a full Certificate. No wonder, his mother was very proud of him.

"How I wish your father was here to share in our joy," his mother told him, looking up at a picture of Balkisoon hanging on the wall of the small room serving as lounge and dining-room. "I'm sure he must have been praying for your success."

Every day, the young man listened to the news on the old radio set sitting lamentably on a shelf. He was impatiently waiting for recruitment in the Police Force to be advertised.

About a month and a half after he obtained his exam results, the long awaited announcement came over the air: "*Application to join the Mauritius Police Force is now open. Holders of a School Certificate and of a Higher School Certificate, aged 18 and above, are invited to apply. Be advised, however, that priority will be given to those holding a full Higher School Certificate*".

Holders of a Higher School Certificate might, indeed, become Cadet Inspectors, thus earning a higher salary than an ordinary Constable.

In addition to their academic qualifications, candidates would have to undergo measurement and medical tests. As he had a solid Higher School Certificate and an excellent track record in sports, Ramesh easily found himself among the chosen candidates.

When he was admitted to the Police Training School, however, he experienced a mixed feeling of pride and sorrow. Pride for obvious reasons – the uniform, the position, the status; sorrow for his poor mother. Indeed, during the whole duration of his training, he would have to sleep in the barracks during the week, thus away from his mother. They would, thus, both miss each other.

"I'm really sorry, Mum," he said. "You'll be left all alone by yourself on week days."

"Oh, Ram, don't worry. Your mum will be able to look after herself. Your training must be your priority, son."

Drawing closer to her son, she added: "I'll be missing you, too, Ram. But that's a sacrifice we must accept to make. Unfortunately, on this earth, we obtain nothing for nothing."

That wise saying of his mother reminded Ramesh of a French proverb he had learned at school: "*On ne peut faire d'omelette sans casser d'oeuf.*"[6]

Their satisfaction, however, would be to see each other during weekends. Anyway, time passes very quickly. It flies, in fact. Soon, Ramesh's training would be over. He would, then, be posted at a regional police station and they would meet every day.

While Ramesh was at the Police Training School, his mother kept working at her little business. However, it was not easy for her to do everything y herself. But she did her best.

At night, her ageing body ached with pain. Often, she went to bed without having dined. Not only was she tired, but she didn't feel like cooking only for her. Gradually she started pining. She lost the beauty her husband so admired and protected.

As a result of her impaired health, she could no longer work as hard as she had been working so far. Often, she didn't feel like going to her stall. Consequently, the

---

[6] We cannot make an omelette without cracking the egg's shell.

newspaper editors stopped giving her newspapers to sell.

===============================

Fortunately, after three years of solid training, Ramesh passed his final police exam. He received his police certificate and uniform. No wonder his mother was overjoyed and proud. Her son was now going to join the active Police Force and will be assigned duties.

In a corner of their yard, stood a little shrine surmounted with a red flag floating from a tall bamboo stick. Inside the shrine sat a Hindu goddess clad in a yellow sari, arms crossed.

Sunita thought she should give thanks to the deity for her son's success. She went to buy a coconut, a couple of lemons and an incense stick. On her way back from the shop, she picked a few yellow flowers growing y the road side.

Having taken a bath, she let her long greying hair - still wet - hang down. Standing in front of the shrine, she lit the incense stick and stood it in a glass which she placed before the deity. Then, she rang a little bell while reciting prayers in Hindi. She cracked the coconut by throwing it against a rock with all her force and placed the two halves and the lemons before the deity. Arms crossed, she "chanted" a few words in Hindi. To end the ritual, she peeled off the petals of the yellow flowers and threw them like confetti in the direction of the goddess. Her spiritual duty accomplished, she went back to her chores.

A pass out parade was going to be held at the "*Champ de Mars*"[7] for the new police recruits. That was going to be their official induction in the force.

---

[7] A two-hundred-year-old horse racing track in Port-Louis, the capital of Mauritius.

The recruits' parents were invited to attend the ceremony. High government and police officials would be present. Medals and certificates were going to be presented to the most deserving recruits. The Police Music band would perform. In short, it was going to be a very pompous ceremony!

"Make sure you soon get better, Mum," Ramesh told his mother. "You must absolutely be present for that ceremony."

"Of course, I won't miss that, son. I've been waiting for that day since long."

It was a sunny Saturday in September. The sky over the capital was azure blue. A cool breeze as lowing from the harbour nearby. The national flag was proudly floating. A large marquee had been erected.

The front rows were occupied by very important personalities. The middle seat was occupied by the Prime Minister, smartly dressed in a marine blue suit. On his right sat the Commissioner of Police. About half a dozen shiny medals, hanging from colourful ribbons, adorned his breast. On the left of the Prime Minister, was the President of the

Republic. Further to the left, sat the Prime Minister's wife, robed in a close fitting orange sari. She was, actively, engaged in a conversation with the President's wife.

The other front seats were occupied by Ministers, Members of Parliament and high rank police officers.

Further back, were the parents and relatives of the recruits. Dressed in the red sari that she kept for special occasions, Sunita solemnly sat. A red flower adorned her long greying hair, neatly combed.

On the ground, the Police Music band stood to the maestro's attention. The new recruits were elegantly lined up - the males on one side, the females on the other. How they looked smart in their new dark blue uniform and their well-polished black boots that shone under the bright sun!

At eleven sharp, the ceremony began. The maestro gave the signal and the band burst into a military march. The wind instruments flared; the drums resounded; the cymbals rang.

The parade began. The new recruits marched, beating the ground with their boots. Heads lifted, they marched, looking fixedly at some invisible and immaterial thing ahead of them.

After the parade, the recruits lined up, facing the marquee. The Prime Mister, the President of the Republic and the Commissioner of Police were, each, escorted by a Police Officer of high rank to review the parade.

Sunita made sure she didn't miss anything. She gesticulated in her seat so as not to lose sight of her son. The three personalities began to review the recruits. They stopped before each of them, shaking hands with them to welcome them into the force.

Sunita stretched her neck and spotted Ramesh in the line. How proud she was when she saw her son parading in his impeccable blue uniform! How smart he looked! When the three personalities stopped before him and shook his hand, her pride rose higher.

She couldn't help shedding a tear. Fishing for her handkerchief, she sighed: "Oh Kissoon, Kissoon, how I wish you were here to witness this!"

After the review, the Prime Minister – also Minister of Interior Affairs – addressed a speech to the recruits. He laid much emphasis on the huge responsibility resting upon them. They had to be loyal to the force, do their job without fear or favour and serve and protect the population.

Then the Commissioner of Police also delivered a speech. He repeated a few points mentioned by the Prime Minister. Furthermore, he reminded the recruits of the dangers and risks to which they might be - or would be - exposed while exercising their duty. Criminals and drug-traffickers, especially, represented a potential source of danger. In conclusion, he thanked and congratulated the recruits' parents for their dedication in having brought up their children and "offering" their sons and daughters to the population.

But the best moment was still to come. Indeed, after all the speeches had been delivered, the Commissioner of Police walked up to the microphone and made the following announcement:

"Mr. President, Mr. Prime Minister, distinguished guests, ladies and gentlemen, I am proud to tell you that, during those past three years, our trainees have demonstrated rigid discipline and real dedication in their training. However, one trainee has been really exemplary. His performance has been frankly outstanding. I am honoured to ask His Excellency the President of the Republic to present him with the best Recruit's Medal. That trainee is … Constable Ramesh Ramghuny!"

When the Prime Minister, flanked by the Commissioner of Police, walked up to Ramesh, shook his hand and pinned the Medal to his lapel, thunderous applause burst in the Champ de Mars. Sunita's joy grew to such a height that she nearly fainted. Tears of joy welled up in her eyes.

"Oh Kissoon," she sobbed, "wherever you may be, I thank you for having prayed for our dear son … You can now really rest in peace… Your son's success is also the fruit of your love and hard work."

That night, to celebrate her son's success, Sunita prepared a special meal. She cooked a chicken curry, made mashed potatoes, a lettuce salad and a hot salted fish and tomato chutney.

Before taking dinner, mother and son offered a prayer at the shrine in the yard.

Seated at table, just before beginning to eat, Sunita looked up at Kissoon's picture on the wall: "Thank you, Kissoon. Thank you for your contribution to our son's success."

"Thank you, Dad," added Ramesh, turning towards the picture, "I'll never forget your affection and sacrifice for me. I'll give my best in my jo to make you proud."

And the two sat down to enjoy their dinner.

# CHAPTER 7

## THE STREET MERCHANTS

Bright and determined as he was, Ramesh made rapid progress in the Police Force. He was obedient, punctual, disciplined and hard-working. Very early, he attracted his superiors' attention. As there was an examination to be held for the promotion of constables to the grade of Sergeant, Ramesh set to work, determined to secure that promotion. He had a clear picture of the hierarchy in the police organization. He knew that the grade of Sergeant was the next rung on the ladder. If he managed to get there, that would give him greater confidence to reach greater heights.

Indeed, when the examination results fell, Ramesh's name was on the list of those to be promoted. He, in fact, ranked third on a list of fifty. What an achievement! No wonder his mother was very proud of him! She was convinced her son was well set to make a successful career in the Police Force.

Now that he was a Sergeant, he earned a better salary. He could better help his mother. They had better food to eat. But, prudent and foreseeing, his mother advised caution.

"Be wise with your money, son. Life is getting harder every day. Remember, sooner or later, you will have to get married and raise a family. You will need to buy a plot of land and build your own house. You know quite well that girls getting married nowadays no longer want to live with their -in-laws. They want to have their own house."

As Ramesh listened attentively, his mother laughed and added, "Mothers-in-law, they say, are not easy to live with."

As she laughed, she exposed her edentate mouth. It was then that Ramesh realized what damage age and hard work were causing to his mother. Focused on his career in the police, he had not noticed how his mother was growing lean and weak.

No longer able to get up early and stand on her feet to prepare Indian fries or sell vegetables at her stall, she had begun to sell some vegetables and herbs in certain strategic places. However, she said nothing about that to her son. She knew that he would never allow her do such a thing. He would find that too much for her health. Besides, he was now earning a decent salary. So she could stay at home, do the most important chores and rest. It was of the utmost importance that she take care of her health.

However, she wanted to earn a little extra money to alleviate the financial pressure on her son. She wanted him to save some money for his own use and for his future marriage project.

So, when he was on duty, she would secretly take her vegetable basket and go out to work. However, she always made sure she returned home before her son.

Along with other merchants, she would place herself, with her basket, at bus terminals, near restaurants, or at busy traffic centres to sell a few vegetables. Those street merchants were particularly busy in the afternoon, after working hours. Housewives would flock around them to buy whatever they needed to fix a quick dinner. Sometimes the vegetables were sold peeled, cleaned and cut in small bite-pieces – which was a great advantage for the busy housewives.

However, those street merchants were not very popular among the licensed traders. They paid no license fee, no tax, sold their goods at much lower prices, thus robbing the regular traders of their income. In addition, they locked the entrance to regular outlets.

That started with vegetable merchants. But, seeing the potential in street selling, all kinds of hawkers had followed suit. In fact, one could find all sorts of wares and products in the streets. Apart from vegetables, one could find fruits, canned drinks, sun-glasses, pirated CD alums, T-shirts, jeans, wound plasters, electrical plugs and sockets and you name it!

But the greatest demands were at the gastronomic level. Mauritians are great consumers of fast food. Aware of the great potential in that field, many people had converted to street merchants.

Thus, there were merchants selling Indian cakes – chilly bites, samosas and fried read - cooked in boiling oil – right there, on street pavements.

*"Dhall puri"*[8] sellers made very good money because this is very consistent food: two pairs – or sometimes just one pair – can easily replace a full meal!

Another food in high demand is fish balls and meat balls. Originally Chinese specialties, these have become so popular that people of every ethnic origin have stepped into this activity.

Another great demand is for *"biryani"*. This is a Muslim specialty made with basmati rice cooked with potatoes and beef or fish or chicken. What is attractive with this food is its uniquely exotic aroma due to saffron thread seasoning.

---

[8] A flat and thin bread of yellow colour stuffed with dhall, baked on a hot iron and eaten with vegetable curry, pickles and chutney wrapped inside.

The most popular ones, however, are those who sell a hot soup with pulses and mutton, called "*halim*". That hot spicy soup, sold in plastic bowls, and served with bread, is particularly appreciated in winter when factory and building site workers yearn for a quick warm-up after a hard day's work. Some would even gulp down two or three bowls!

"*Dhall puris*" and "*halim*"[9], especially, are so popular that some merchants have become very wealthy thanks to their trade. One "*halim*" merchant even goes to work, driving in his ... red convertible Mercedes! He often ostensibly posts his picture on Facebook. Of course, he takes another car to transport his "*halim*" and other utensils. The convertible drives only the ... boss!

The proliferation of those street merchants soon became a nuisance. Shopkeepers and market vegetable sellers began to protest. They wrote letters of complaint to the municipal authorities, asking them to take

---

[9] A spicy soup of pulses and mutton eaten hot with bread.

sanctions. While they had patents and taxes to pay, the street merchants were unlicensed and, thus, in illegality. Why should they be allowed to have a free ride?

Nor were those the only problems they caused. Members of the public and road users also expressed their grievances. Indeed, because of the activities of those hawkers, it was becoming more and more difficult for pedestrians to use street pavements and for motorists to drive safely. Traffic jams were becoming a major problem.

It was no longer a matter of nipping the serpent in the bud: the viper had already hatched!

# CHAPTER 8

## ENTER OFFICER JEEWANSING

Ramesh passed promotional exams one after another. His field performance also was exemplary and won him his superiors' appreciation. He demonstrated a real determination to combat criminality and had many arrests to his name. Soon his name began to instil fear in potential malefactors. He became a deterrent against crime.

He made such great and rapid progress that four years after his induction into the Police Force, he had reached the grade of Inspector. He had, one day, led a squadron on a dangerous mission aimed at dismantling a vast drug-trafficking cartel. During the attack, he had narrowly escaped death: a gun shot missed him by a hair's breadth! But the

Head of the cartel – one "Black Tiger" – was arrested and jailed. As a result of that catch, Ramesh was awarded the Police Meritorious Achievement Medal.

Thanks to his outstanding achievements and quick ascension, Ramesh was given charge of a Police station. He had a team of twelve officers – eight male and four female - under his command. He was very rigid and did not tolerate the least default on the part of his subordinates.

One day, a police jeep drove into the yard of the station where Ramesh worked. A Sergeant walked into the station, followed by a very beautiful young lady officer. They were shown into Ramesh's office. The young man was impressed by the beauty of that lady officer so smartly dressed in her impeccable uniform.

Taking off his cap and saluting Ramesh, the Sergeant said: "Inspector, please meet Officer Sweta Jeewansing." Then, turning towards the lady officer, he added: "Officer Jeewansing, please meet Inspector Ramghuny."

"Pleased to meet you, Officer," said Ramesh, shaking hands with the lady."

"Officer Jeewansing," the Sergeant resumed, "is being transferred from Rocky Hill station to your station." And, saying this, he handed a sealed envelope to Ramesh.

"Officer," the Sergeant said, turning to the lady, "as from today and until further notice, you'll be attached to this station and you'll be under Inspector Ramghuny's command."

"Welcome into our team, Officer Jeewansing," said Ramesh. I'm sure that, with your collaboration and your input, we'll do a wonderful job tracking those criminals."

"You can rest assured, Inspector, that I'll give you my full support."

"Indeed," said the Sergeant, "Officer Jeewansing is a very dedicated member of the force. You'll have, in her, a very loyal team member. She's being transferred because we're already overstaffed at Rocky Hill. With the rising number of women lawbreakers in this region, her service will be much needed here."

Indeed, prostitution and drug addiction are ruining the lives of many here," conceded Inspector Ramghuny. "Officer Jeewansing's help will be much appreciated," he added turning to the lady officer with a smile.

"I wish you a good and fruitful collaboration for the welfare of our citizens," said the Sergeant. "I'd better go now. Plenty of work waiting for me at Rocky Hill."

He shook hands with both, put on his cap and left.

Turning to the lady officer, Inspector Ramghuny said: "Do take a seat at that desk and rest a while. Make yourself at home. Most of our officers are out on duty now. Tomorrow morning, I'll introduce you to the whole team. You have a couple of issues of *"The Detective"* on the desk. You may take a look."

As the lady officer walked to the desk she had been shown, Ramesh admired her elegance. He took a thick file, opened it and flipped the pages forward and backward, pretending to be searching for some entry - an entry which, he knew, never was entered.

In reality, every now and then, he cast a glance in her direction. He was like a heliotrope, irresistibly turning towards the sun.

She was aged about twenty-three, had clear complexion and beautiful brown eyes. Her dyed hair was cut shoulder length. She seemed to be out of place in that old building whose colour had long fainted.

Sometimes, when Ramesh lifted his head to steal a glance at her, he noticed that she was playing the same game as he. Disconcerted, they would then sketch a smile.

But, Ramesh was soon reminded of his duty. Conscientious as he was, he kept their relationship at professional level. Maybe later he might consider otherwise. He still had a lot more to achieve. He had to build his own house before contemplating wedlock.

A French proverb he remembered from his high school days says: *"Beaucoup d'eau devra couler sous le pont..."*[10]

On the following morning, before assigning their tasks to his subordinates, Inspector Ramghuny convened a meeting with them.

"I have called this brief meeting," he told them, "to assign to each your duty. But, let me inform you that, since yesterday, there is a new member on our staff."

A few throat clearings could be heard among the female officers.

"I would like you to welcome among us another lady officer in the person of ..."

A few more throat clearings from the womenfolk. But Inspector Ramghuny was no dupe. He understood that that was an expression of jealousy because the newcomer's beauty couldn't have escaped them. He only hoped that it was just instinctive and that it wouldn't last long, thus

---

[10] Literal translation: Much water will have to flow under the bridge.

hampering their efficiency as a team. Anyway, should that happen, he knew how to deal with the situation. He wouldn't allow feminine jealousy or envy or whim to get in their way: he was determined to take sanctions against any offender – whoever she might be.

"I would like you," he resumed, "to welcome in our midst a new lady officer in the person of Officer Jeewansing. She's just been transferred from Rocky Hill station. I trust you will continue to work as a team and with increased determination to eradicate the drug and prostitution plague in the region. Remember that law and order must be our number one priority and that everything else – yes eve…ry…thing else – must be set aside so that our service to the community gets our full and unreserved attention."

He purposely stretched the "eve …ry…thing" to make it clear he had suspected some ill feeling among the womenfolk. In addition, while pronouncing that word, he had intently moved his gaze towards them and fixed it on them.

"Now," he said, concluding the meeting, "let's see what's awaiting us today…"

And, taking a big log book, he began attributing duties.

Quite fortunately, as days went by, work went well. Collaboration – vertical as well as horizontal – went on smoothly. Even on the personal level, Officer Jeewansing and the other lady officers got on very well. The male officers were very courteous and supportive - offering assistance and advice whenever required.

Inspector Ramghuny was fully satisfied with his team. He was convinced that, with everybody's collaboration, the area would soon be rid of evil doers and that the inhabitants would be able to live in a safe and secure environment.

# CHAPTER 9

## PANIC AT THE POLICE STATION

One Wednesday, at around ten, a lady rushed inside the station. She was evidently in a state of panic. Dishevelled, sweating and panting, she asked an officer: "Quick! Can I meet the person in charge?"

She was clearly in a state of shock. Something wrong and serious must have happened to her.

"Sure, ma'am" the panicking officer answered, knocking on the Inspector's door.

But the lady's attitude changed briskly and radically when her gaze fell on the copper plate on the door: it read: "Inspector Ramesh Ramghuny, Officer-in-Charge".

Before the door opened, she stammered: "I'm sorry … I'm sorry, officer …"

And she rushed out of the station much more quickly than she had rushed in.

Having heard the knock and hearing the din, but seeing nobody entering, Ramesh briskly opened the door.

"What's the matter, Officer?" he enquired.

"A lady, Inspector," the officer answered, trying to explain, "a lady rushed in, wanted to see you, then …"

As he pointed towards the door, Ramesh rushed to look outside.

About five metres away, he saw a dishevelled woman running across the street amidst a concert of car horns. He had no difficulty recognizing the woman: Leela, his insufferable aunt!

But what was the matter with her? What had happened to her? Why was she on foot and not in her Mercedes? Why did she want to see me? And why had she left in such a rush?

Such were the many questions that crossed Ramesh's mind as he silently and slowly walked back to his office.

Soon he dismissed his thoughts and resumed his work. That morning, he was looking into a thick report on one of the problems that were plaguing the region. He was trying to devise a strategy to close down all the brothels and fake massage salons and put all pimps and prostitutes behind prison bars.

On the following morning, on his way to the station, he bought the daily *"The Morning Messenger"*. As soon as he sat at his desk, he opened the paper to read the front page news. A title in block letters attracted his attention: "A MERCEDES CAR VANDALIZED – LADY DRIVER MOLESTED!"

Curious to get the details, he began to read the article:

*"Yesterday, in Presidency street, Quatre-Bornes, a black Mercedes car, plate number GR 456-2496, was vandalized in broad daylight. The lady driver, Mrs. L.R, was molested while trying to stop the vandals who ran away with her brand new iPhone*

*and her handbag containing her I.D card, all her debit and credit cards and a sum of R78,000. Passers-y say they saw a woman running like mad across the streets, searching for help ...*"

The car's make, the letters GR on the plate number, the initials L.R confirmed unmistakably that it was the panic-stricken woman who had acted so bizarrely in the station the day before - his antipathetic and vain aunt – Leela Ramghuny, wife of Gopal Ramghuny.

But why had she rushed into the station, seeking for assistance and run away like mad before receiving help?

After turning and re-turning that question in his mind, Ramesh thought he had found the answer.

"Yes," he said to himself, "it must be that! I can see no other reason. Pride, vanity, shame! She couldn't bear to be helped by somebody she so despised! How could she – that rich and vain bourgeoise – beg for assistance from me, Ramesh, a vegetable planter's son? She must have been mad with anger seeing my name on the door. She who tried to persuade me to abandon my studies, seeing my position now …"

Then, after a pause and coming out of his pensive mood, he added: "Anyway, had she asked for help, I would have given her all the assistance required. It's my duty, after all, and I have sworn an oath to that effect."

Just then the telephone on his desk rang. Picking it up, he concluded: "Well, that was her choice."

Yes, Inspector Ramghuny here …"

# CHAPTER 10

## POLICE STREET OPERATION

One Tuesday afternoon in October, Inspector Ramesh Ramghuny's police station was called: a fierce quarrel had broken out between shop owners and restaurant keepers against street merchants!

"Hurry up, Inspector Ramghuny," commanded the Assistant-Commissioner over the phone. "I've got news they're brandishing sabres and knives! It appears there are casualties, too! Take a squadron under your command and rush to the junction of Queen Victoria and William Shakespeare streets! Put those ruffians under arrest!"

At once, Ramesh assembled his ablest officers, fastened his belt, making sure his revolver was in its holster. He jumped into a jeep and, followed by two other jeeps, rushed to the spot where the brawl had broken. Officer Sweta Jeewansing got into one of the jeeps following.

When the mob heard the police sirens whizzing and wailing, they rushed in all directions. Some, in their mad flight, dropped their weapons, which lay scattered on the asphalt. A wounded man lay screaming with pain in the middle of the road, all his plastic wares scattered around him. Baskets of vegetables had been abandoned. Beetroots, potatoes and carrots were rolling down the street. Tomatoes, trampled underfoot, had turned into ketchup. The road was smeared with blood.

All kinds of wares, products and vegetables lay helter-skelter, littering the streets. Here and there, amidst all that dirt, were a few coins and crumpled bank notes which had been dropped in the panic.

The *"dholl puri"* merchants got into the saddle – some cycling and others pedaling away as fast as they could. Only the Indian cake sellers, the biryani merchants and the *"halim"* merchants remained on the spot. They were not involved in the brawl and, besides, their food stuff and utensils were too cumbersome for them to attempt a quick escape.

Judging by the mess on the road, it was easy to know that those directly involved were the vegetable and general wares sellers.

"Come on," shouted Inspector Ramghuny to his officers. "Hurry and get them!"

At once, the officers armed with bludgeons, chased the mob. Some were caught and handcuffed; others were overpowered and brutally dumped into the jeeps.

Officer Jeewansing and two other lady officers participating in the crackdown operation arrested a few women sellers. As they were made to get into the police vehicles, they begged for mercy.

"Excuse us, officers," they pleaded, "have mercy. We were merely trying to earn a few rupees."

Others cried: "We've got kids at home. They need food. Please, let us go."

But the officers remained unflinching.

As for the men arrested, they tried to resist force and cursed. But they were finally handcuffed and pushed into the jeeps.

Inspector Ramghuny did not personally participate in the arrests. As Officer-in-charge, he stood there, his revolver in his hand, and shouted orders to his officers. The latter ran in all directions, chasing the law-breakers around street corners, into people's yards and into shops where they tried to take refuge.

"Look, there's one there hiding among those cartons!" yelled Inspector Ramghuny, noticing a movement about thirty metres away.

One of his men rushed to the spot towards which pointed the Inspector's finger. A woman, who had been squatting there, rushed out of her hideout and ran down the road like mad. The police officer kept at her heels. The woman ran as fast as a deer, her sari falling off and her long hair undone. The officer, himself, was panting, trying to catch up with her.

But, suddenly something happened: the strap of one of the woman's rubber flip flops broke! She missed a step, her foot trampled the hem of her sari and she fell heavily on the asphalt with a loud noise.

Panic-stricken, Inspector Ramghuny rushed to the spot. Bending down, he passed one arm under the woman's body to lift it off the hard surface. With the other hand, he lifted the top of the woman's sari that had fallen over her face.

As he did so, he got the shock of his life: two tearful eyes stared him in the face – those of his mother! Blood was oozing out of her mouth. Laying the lifeless body down, the Inspector fell flat on it, weeping his eyes out under the stunned gaze of all his petrified officers.

"My mum," he cried, "oh, my mum, my dear mummy! I've killed my mum!"

Still his men didn't quite understand. How could they suspect their Inspector's mother was an illegal street merchant? Not even did *he*, the Inspector, know!

"That's my mother, my beloved mother!" he wept, turning to his men. "Do you understand? That's my poor mum and I've killed her! I'm cursed now!"

His face bathing in tears, he sobbed and wept like a child. And, indeed, he was for that now lifeless mass of flesh lost in her loose sari.

As he closed her eyelids, the Inspector noticed that she held something in her clenched hand. Pulling it open, he found a small cloth bag. When he opened it, his tears fell like a river on his dead mother's face: the bag contained a few coins and two wrinkled bank notes totaling R180.50 – one hundred and eighty rupees and fifty cents! Those were her very last earnings! Behind the cartons where she had been hiding, they found her basket: in it, about half a dozen beetroots, a few carrots, some tomatoes, and a few bunches of thyme and parsley.

"Oh, Mum," he lamented, "why did you have to do that? Why didn't you tell me?"

Meanwhile, a crowd had gathered around the Inspector. Some were sympathizing with him Others began to shout in anger and in unison: "Criminal! Murderer! Criminal! Murderer! Shame on the police!"

Newspaper reporters had rushed to the spot, too. Their camera flashes crackled. They questioned the bystanders and scribbled notes in small notebooks. They asked for a statement from the Inspector, but his officers moved them away.

An ambulance was summoned. It soon arrived, its sirens blaring. The officers had a hard time trying to disperse the crowd. The woman's dead body was placed on a stretcher and pushed into the ambulance which drove at full speed to John F. Kennedy Hospital for an autopsy.

Once he was back at the station, Inspector Ramghuny took off his cap, removed his belt, took his revolver out of its holster and threw them on his desk.

He then sat down, switched on the slow desk computer sitting lazily in a corner and started typing. When he had finished, he took off his uniform and dressed into the plain clothes he always had at the station. Calling a police courier, he ordered him thus:

"Officer, quickly get into one of our vehicles and take this letter, special dispatch, to the Commissioner's office at headquarters."

His letter read thus:


"To the Commissioner of Police,

Police Headquarters.

17 October, 19..


Sir,

I regret to have to submit my resignation from the Police Department.

Today, during a police crack-down to track street merchants, I caused my dear mother's death. I acknowledge the fact that she was acting illegally. But her sole and legitimate aim was to help me pursue my education and my career. I owe my success to her and to her activity – illegal or not.

But, I am proud to say that all she was doing was selling a few vegetables – not drugs or pornographic materials or pirated CD alums like many bothers do.

I am sorry I can no longer associate myself with a police that killed my mother and that tracks poor people who are sacrificing themselves for their families.

Excuse my naivety, but I had always thought there were the law *and* the spirit of the law. That's what I had been told during my training.

I thank you for the time I was allowed to serve in the Police Department. I hope you will understand my position and the reason for my decision. Some will consider it irrational and ill-inspired. But criminals' place is, you will agree, *not* in the police.

And I feel like I am one now.

Yours respectfully,

Ramesh Ramghuny.

(Signed).

===================================

Thus, against all odds and for reasons no-one would have ever suspected, Inspector Ramesh Ramghuny voluntarily put an end to a long-desired and successful career in the Police Department.

On the next day, the incident made front page news:


"POLICE INSPECTOR'S MOTHER KILLED DURING POLICE OPERATION LED BY SAME INSPECTOR!"

# CHAPTER 11

## REVISITING THE PLANTATION

Six months after those tragic incidents, Ramesh's mourning of his mother was over. For about one month, he had eaten only vegetables. Every Sunday morning, he had gone to the cemetery where his mother's ashes had been buried. He brought offerings of apples and oranges which he ceremoniously placed on the tomb. He sometimes brought a coconut which he cracked on a stone and placed on the tomb. At night, before going to bed, he lit an oil lamp in front of a picture of his late father and mother, that sat on a shelf above his bed.

Without his father and his mother, he felt very lonesome. The house was cold and silent now. Sometimes, he didn't feel like cooking. He would, then, buy a loaf and a banana or a pair of "*dholl puris*" which, taken with a cup of tea, constituted his meal. He no longer switched on the radio. He had developed a hatred for it since he had learned that it had announced the fatal event as "Breaking News" minutes after it took place. He couldn't bear the idea that the whole population was now aware of what he called his "parricide".

He was even reluctant to go out into the streets. Whenever he did, people turned round to look at him, murmuring in one another's ear. If he went to the regional shop or to the barber's, people questioned him about the incident or made some sort of embarrassing allusion to it.

One day, feeling particularly nostalgic, he went to his late father's plantation. All its green luxuriance had vanished. It had fallen in ruins. A few vegetables had withered and turned yellow. The sun and the absence of irrigation had completely damaged it. Weeds had invaded it. Rats and mongooses fed on the rotten vegetables. Carcasses lay here and there. A fetid smell aggressed the nose.

At the far end of the plantation, stood a mango tree. During the fruit season, his father had, on a few occasions, brought a few mangoes home.

As a child, Ramesh, too, had sometimes accompanied his father to the plantation when mangoes were in season. On such occasions, he had, himself, climbed into the tree to pick mangoes. He would sit up on a branch and eat a few before climbing down to take the others home. While Ramesh enjoyed the juicy yellow flesh of the ripe fruits, his mother liked better the green ones which she used to make hot spicy chutney and pickles.

That mango tree must have sheltered his father from the summer heat. He pictured the old man sitting in its shade to take his meal, then lying down to take a short rest before resuming his work.

But now the tree had begun to wither. The few leaves on it had turned yellow and crispy. Its dry and rare branches protruded from the tired trunk like long arms lamentably begging for water.

Threading his way amidst all that filth, Ramesh went to the old cabin in which his father took his lunch and kept his implements. The iron sheet door creaked on its rusty hinges as he pulled it open.

On the floor, he found a piece of bread that had gathered mold and an empty plastic bottle. Vestiges of his father's last lunch at the plantation! In a corner lay a pile of raffia bags and, under it, a long rope. Ramesh guessed his father must have used those bags to hold his vegetables when he prepared them for delivery to the hotels.

But, as for the rope, he couldn't think of a satisfying explanation for its presence there. Unless he used it to tie the vegetable bags so he could more easily pull them or haul them …

But, just then, a few small brown paper wrappers on the floor attracted his attention. They seemed to have been torn open hastily and carelessly.

Picking one up, Ramesh read the inscription on it: *"Aspirin"*!

He never knew his father took Aspirin. He didn't think his mother knew either. His father had never complained of any health issue at home, that required medication. He had, of course, suffered from the seasonal 'flu like anybody else. But that was easily cured by administration of old folk medicine which his mother knew quite well how to prepare.

The old man, Ramesh reflected, must have suffered from some rather serious health problem but had kept it to himself so as not to alarm his wife and his son.

Ramesh's eyes filled with tears. The thought that his father had been killing himself toiling in the plantation for his academic success was unbearable. He felt twice guilty for having, in one way or another, been responsible for his parents' deaths.

The young man sat down on a large rock protruding from the ground. Holding his hand in his cupped hands, he soon fell into a pensive mood. All kinds of images crossed his mind. The longer he remained in that mood, the deeper he plunged and the darker the pictures on his internal movie screen.

Suddenly, he couldn't bear it any longer. He got out of his torpor and shook his head as if to exorcize those dark thoughts.

With a determined step, he went to the little cabin, dry leaves crackling under his feet. He flung the door open, bent down and grabbed the rope.

With long strides, he made for the mango tree. Holding one end of the rope between his teeth, he looked for a firm grip and began to climb into the tree. His first two trials failed. His hands slipped and hurt as they rubbed against the rough trunk.

Finally, he managed to get a foothold on a short but solid ranch. Stretching one arm, he got hold of a branch higher up. From then on, his climb became easier. From one branch, he reached for another and then to another.

Finally, he was high up enough. Looking down, he saw a thick layer of dry leaves and few stones sticking out here and there.

He took the end of the rope out of his mouth, flung it over a thick protruding branch, rolled it a few times around the branch and made a couple of very tight knots. He then pulled on the rope to test the solidity of the knots.

When he was satisfied they held good, he pulled up a reasonable length of rope and began to make a loop which he passed around his neck …

Suddenly a big branch broke and fell heavily with a loud noise on the carpet of dry leaves. At the same time, a voice shouted:

"Hey there! What are you doing?"

Looking in the direction from where the voice came, he saw a feminine figure. "It" came running at full speed, stumbled, recovered its balance and shouted: "Oh, my God! Stop! Don't do that!"

When Ramesh looked down, he saw Officer Sweta Jeewansing, looking up, horrified. Dressed in plain clothes, she wore tight green jeans, a light green silk blouse and white sneakers with a green band at the back. She looked very athletic.

That was the first time Ramesh saw her in plain clothes. In her uniform at the station, she looked like just any other officer – except for her undeniable beauty. But, now, dressed in green in that agricultural environment, she really stood out!

"What are you doing up there in that tree and what's that rope for?" she asked, looking anxious.

Of course, as a police officer, she perfectly knew what he was up to. When she was posted at Rocky Hill, she had once been dispatched with two colleagues to a wooden house where a body had been found hanging from a beam. It turned out to be a fifty-year old alcoholic, living alone.

"How did you know I was here?" Ramesh asked from his branch, the rope loosely rolled around his neck. "How did you find me?"

"Please, Ramesh," she said, ignoring his questions.

For her, the priority was to get him down that tree and free of that rope.

"Do come down, Ramesh. I beg you to. Then we'll talk."

The desperate young man wondered what to do. Should he climb down or go on with his morbid plan? If he dropped his plan, would he have peace of mind? Would he obtain the redemption he so craved? How long would he be able to live alone in that cold empty house?

On the other hand, if he went ahead with his plan, would he not lose that beauty standing at the foot of the tree, imploring him? Are there such beauties in the afterlife? And, should his soul transmigrate into another body – as he had been told souls did – would their paths cross again? What were the odds?

"Here am I in a Corneillian dilemma![11]" he said to himself.

That was an expression he had learned in high school when he was studying *"Le Cid"*, a tragedy by the 17<sup>th</sup> century French dramatist Pierre Corneille.

As Ramesh went on dilly-dallying, the young lady waited impatiently for him to climb down. He would turn to the branch above his head to which the rope was tied then to the young lady below, wondering what to do.

"Please, Ramesh, for God's sake" she pleaded again, hands crossed: "do take that rope from around your neck and come down. I beg you to!"

Her fear was that, if he missed a step or if he slipped or still if the branch on which he was standing broke, the consequence would be fatal! And she didn't want that to happen! Nor did she want to be witness to that!

---

[11] "Corneillian" is the adjective derived from the name Corneille. A Corneillian dilemma is a situation where one is divided between two conflicting options – such as love and duty.

When he saw the young lady's lips move rapidly as if she was talking softly to somebody, he carefully began to take the loop off his neck. How relieved the young lady was!

"Thank you, Ramesh. Do come down now."

Vanquished by the soft affectionate voice, the tender-hearted young man began his descent, making sure where he put his feet. When he reached the last branch down and was about to touch ground, the young lady drew near to catch and steady him - lest he should miss the ground and fall.

The landing was soft, safe and, especially, satisfying for Sweta!

"Thank you," the young lady said, completely relieved. "Thank you, Ramesh. You nearly made my heart stop."

Holding Ramesh's hand, Miss Jeewansing led him away from the tree. He threw away the rope that fell to the ground like a snake that writhed a while then dropped down, motionless. Ramesh walked, head bent and not saying a word. He felt ashamed that Miss Jeewansing, his former subordinate, had witnessed his moment of weakness and his cowardice. For him, not going to the end of his decision was tantamount to cowardice.

But the perspicacious Miss Jeewansing understood his state of mind.

"Don't feel guilty or ashamed, Ramesh," she said to comfort him. "We are all human. We all have our ups and downs ... And our weaknesses."

Still Ramesh kept quiet. He was pondering over the young lady's wise words like a goat grinding grass.

"I understand your situation, Ram," she said, "you cannot blame yourself for what happened. The fault was not in you, but in the law. Or rather in those who make the law - government."

Ramesh was moved when he heard the young lady call him "Ram". That was the endearing way his father and his mother used to call him in moments of special affection.

"Do you want to sit down and rest a while," she suggested, "before we go away?"

The young man nodded affirmatively.

# CHAPTER 12

## A MOMENT OF INTIMACY

They found a relatively clean spot and sat down. A number of questions arose in Ramesh's mind and he was eager to obtain answers to them.

"You haven't told me yet," he began, "how you knew I was here ..."

"I went to see you at your place ..."

"At my place? But you don't know where I live."

"Oh, I sure do, Ram," she said, smiling. "You must have forgotten. Remember, one day, after work, Sergeant Nanbacchus and I drove you home because we had to pass that way to attend to a call from a woman having trouble with a neighbour."

"Oh, yes," Ramesh said, "I remember now. But how did you happen to find me *here*?" and he stressed the "here".

"When I found your house empty, a neighbour of yours suggested I tried to look for you in your father's plantation and he directed me here."

"Oh, I see. That must be Raymond, the shoemaker. But how come you're not at the station today? You're on leave?"

Miss Jeewansing smiled heartily. "You'll be surprised. I've resigned ..."

"Resigned?" Ramesh asked in shock. "Did I hear clearly?"

"You did, Ram. I've resigned. I'm no longer in the force."

"But why? A right and secure career was awaiting you there ..."

"Listen, Ram," Miss Jeewansing began to explain. "An uncle of mine has just opened a travel agency and, as he travels a lot for his many businesses, he's asked me to take charge of the agency."

"This sounds good, Sweta. You'll now be better off, working for a family member and being in charge without a stupid Inspector to take orders from," Ramesh said, laughing about his joke.

Miss Jeewansing was happy to see that Ramesh was now in a much better mood.

"And how was the mood at the station after I left?" he enquired.

"Well, we were all shocked by what had happened. Nobody expected you to hand over your resignation letter so impulsively. Of course, everybody regretted your departure. You were so professional in your work."

"I also miss you all since I left. But I think I did the right thing. How could I continue applying such merciless laws against poor people working for their living? And how many more poor mothers would I have to kill?"

"To tell you frankly, Ram, that incident at the junction of Queen Victoria and William Shakespeare streets also got me thinking. So, when my uncle offered me that job at his travel agency, I heartily welcomed it."

"You know, Sweta," Ramesh said, sounding perplexed, "there's something that worries me ..."

Showing concern, Sweta drew closer to him. She feared he might relapse into his dark mood.

"What is it, Ram?" she affectionately asked. "You can trust me, dear. Do speak your mind. I'll do my best to help you ... if you allow me to, of course."

"At night, Sweta, it's hard for me to get some sleep. The memory of that fatal day still haunts me. I keep seeing my dead mother's tearful eyes staring at me as if pleading for mercy. Or, was it reproach?"

Tears came to his eyes. "Excuse me," he said, sniffing. He pulled a crumpled brown handkerchief out of his pocket and blew his nose.

"But that won't last forever, Ram. It's quite understandable. Soon you will have forgotten …"

"No, Sweta," Ram protested vehemently. "That's something I'll never forget. How could I ever forget? That's something I'll have to pay for throughout eternity. And, if I ever reincarnate, let me be the most miserable and the most detestable creature walking – no, creeping in the dust!"

"Oh no, Ram. Please, don't say that! Don't mortify yourself. You're a nice guy and a kindhearted one. And intelligent, too. You won't ever reincarnate. Nobody ever does and nobody ever will!"

"But that's what I've been taught, Sweta. That's what the pundit has always told us. My parents believed that and brought me up believing that."

Then a question arose in the young man's mind.

"But don't you believe that, Sweta? Hasn't your pundit told you?"

"Listen, Ram. My parents are of Indian origin and were brought up as devout Hindus. When I was born, I was brought up in the Hindu religion, too…"

"But," broke in Ramesh, "but, you're still Hindu, aren't you? Your name is Sweta Jeewansing – that's Hindu!"

"You're right, Ram. My name is Hindu – just like my parents' names. My father's name is Bisham and my mother's, Devi. But – as they say - what's in a name, Ram? We were all born in the Hindu religion. We performed Hindu rituals, celebrated Hindu feasts and, every year, we went on pilgrimage to the sacred lake. But, when I was fifteen and in secondary school, I fell seriously ill. I developed asthma, was disturbed – tormented even - in my sleep and … excuse me, Ram, but can I tell you that? I had prolonged and irregular menstrual bleeding accompanied by terrible pains."

Ramesh listened attentively to the young lady's candid confession.

"Oh dear," he said compassionately, "you must have suffered terribly!"

"Oh yes, Ram. I often had to miss school, was often taken to the doctor's or to the *"shivala"*[12]. The pundit prayed for me, we made offerings ... My parents even once took me to a witchdoctor who asked for a big sum of money – twenty thousand rupees, if I remember - plus an ox to be sacrificed!"

"You've been through all that, Sweta? the young man asked, sincerely moved by what he heard. "How sad! And did you parents pay the money and offer the ox?"

"You bet they didn't! Of course, we didn't have that much money. And you know the price of an ox?"


"What did they do then? Do you still have those ... what is it called?"

---

[12] Hindu temple.

"Symptoms," she answered, laughing heartily.

"Yes, symptoms. You see, Sweta, I'm losing my faculties." And he laughed, too.

"Well, a colleague of my mother at the garment factory where she worked, one day, gave her a pamphlet. It was titled: *"Jesus said: ""Come to me, all you who labor and are heavily burdened, and I will give you rest""*[13]. We read it attentively and were impressed and interested. It further said: "By *His Stripes You're Healed*[14]". At the end of the message, it said: "**Jesus said to him, "*I am the way, the truth, and the life. No one comes to the Father, except through me.*"[15].**

I can't remember how many times we read and re-read the short but powerful message.

---

[13] Matthew 11:28.

[14] Isaiah 53:5; 1 Peter 2:24.

[15] John 14:6.

Never before had we heard such wonderful words!"

"What you're saying," Ramesh said, clearly impressed, "is, indeed, amazing! I've never heard such words! I don't understand what they mean, but they sound like magic to me. And what did you do next?"

"Well, Ram, on the verso there was a stamped cliché with the name of a church: "Word of Truth Gospel Church". There followed the address, a phone number and the days and times when services were held. When my mother mentioned my health problems to her colleague, she invited my mother to one of their church meetings and asked her to bring me. They had a service on Fridays called "Deliverance Service".

"Deliverance    Service?"    Ram    asked, intrigued. "What's that?"

"Well, on those days, the pastor prayed specially for the sick. After having hesitated some time because of the reactions our relatives might have, my mother took a resolution: 'We just cannot keep on watching you suffer like that and do nothing. We've tried everything possible – doctors, offerings, prayers at the *"shivala"* and even a witch doctor. All to no avail! I just don't care what others say. You're *our* child, Sweta. It's our duty to seek your welfare. This Friday, I'll take you to that Deliverance Service, come what may! Say what they will!"

"Indeed," Sweta continued, "the following Friday, my mother, with my father's consent, took me to the Deliverance Service. There were about two hundred people present. What surprised me was that I had always thought that only people of Creole origin attended that church because they usually pray to Jesus. I had always believed that Jesus was the God of the Creoles. But I was shocked to see people of almost all origins. The number of Hindus and Tamils was impressive."

"When the service began, they all prayed together with a loud voice. Not used to that, I felt afraid. Then they sang beautiful songs about God and Jesus. I really enjoyed the singing. It was loud, but beautiful. Soon, I felt like a warm shivering running down my spine."

As he listened, Ramesh grew more and more eager to know more. He couldn't wait to know the rest.

"After the singing which lasted for about thirty or forty minutes," Sweta continued, "the pastor read a passage from the Bible. Then he preached about the text he had just read. I remember it was about a father asking Jesus to heal his child who was aggressed by a demon. The demon would throw the child into water and into fire to kill him ..."[16]

"How awful!" Ramesh exclaimed. "Demons are real then?"

"Yes, Ramesh. Demons *do* exist! They are *very* real! But listen. When the father brought the child to Jesus, Jesus commanded the demon to leave. The child fell down, like one dead. His mouth foamed. Everybody thought he had died. But Jesus took him by the hand, lifted him up and gave him back to his father – alive! All those present were amazed."

---

[16] Mark 9:17-26.

"Indeed, that's amazing!" Ramesh exclaimed, really impressed. "But what about you, Sweta? What happened to you? I'm curious to know."

"Well, after the preaching, the pastor asked people who needed prayers for healing to come forward. Without hesitation, my mother took me by the hand and brought me forward. Soon we were surrounded by about thirty bother people – men, women, children. The pastor made us repeat a short prayer after him. Then his assistants and himself began laying hands upon the people and paying with authority. I heard them repeat phrases like: *"In the Name of Jesus, the blood of Jesus!"*"

"When the pastor reached me, he asked me to close my eyes. He placed his hands on my head and began to pray. I remember him saying: *'In the Name of Jesus, get out!'* When I reopened my eyes, I found myself lying on the floor. I felt lighter, refreshed – like a weight had been lifted off me. I was covered with a cloth and two women were squatting beside me, praying. They then lifted me up and asked me to say: *'**Thank you, Jesus. I confess you as my Saviour and my Lord. Thank you for healing me.**'* They gave me a little booklet with verses from the Gospel and asked me to read them before going to bed."

"What you're telling me, Sweta," Ramesh said, "is quite strange. I've never heard anything like this before! And what happened to you next?"

"Well, I read the little booklet every night before going to ed. Strange enough, Ram, since that Friday night after the Deliverance Service, I've been sleeping soundly. No more torment, no more nightmare …"

"And your asthma?"

"Gone, Ramesh, gone!"

"Amazing!" exclaimed the young man, whistling his surprise.

"From then on, I've been breathing normally. I pursued my studies like any other student. Oh, I forgot to tell you, my menstrual problem also is gone."

"That's a miracle!" exclaimed Ramesh.

"You've named it, Ramesh. A miracle and nothing less."

"But do you still go to that church?"

"Oh yes, Ramesh. Seeing my miraculous healing, my mother took me regularly to that church. Not only on Fridays, though. We soon began to attend the Tuesday and Sunday services, as well. On Tuesdays, they gave Bible teachings and, on Sundays, they spent more time on worshipping God with music and singing. I particularly enjoyed the Sunday services. Sometimes a pastor from another church came to preach from the Bible. Ah, will you believe me, Ram, one Sunday, I was shocked to see a pastor of Hindu origin coming for the preaching. He was called Pastor Kishore. The way he preached, quoting Bible verses, you'd say he was born Christian! On Sundays, they also broke read and serve the pieces and a little wine to the believers ..."

"Bread and wine, you say, Sweta?" Ramesh asked.

"Oh, just a little piece of bread and a sip of wine. They called that the 'Lord's Supper'. Jesus did that with his disciples before they took Him to die on the cross."

"What about your father? Did he accompany you, too?"

"When he saw my healing and the change in my mother – she had become more caring, more affectionate – my father soon began to accompany us. After some time, he quit drinking and smoking altogether. Not that he had been a drunkard – oh no, Ram – he would every now and then take a drink or two. Now he's teetotal, praise God."

"Formidable!" Ramesh exclaimed.

"Indeed, Ram. About three months later, my father, my mother and myself openly confessed Jesus Christ as our Saviour and Lord, and were baptized in water ..."

"Baptized? What do you mean?"

"Well, Jesus also was baptized when He lived on earth. He didn't need to. But He set an example for us to follow. When we are baptized, we identify ourselves with Him."

"Excuse me for asking so many questions, Sweta. But what about your relatives – aunts, uncles, cousins …?"

"Oh, Ram, they were not happy. Their attitude towards us has changed since. But we don't care. What matters is our well-being. And most of all, we have eternal life in Jesus."

"Eternal life?" Ramesh asked, frowning. "What do you mean, Sweta?"

"That's the best gift we have through Jesus, Ram. One day, when we die, we shall go on to live forever with Jesus in Heaven. There will no longer be any disease, any misery, any problem and no more death …"

"But how come you know all that, Sweta? Is everything you're saying true?"

"That's in the Bible, Ram. It's God's Word. And God doesn't lie. Jesus has made the promise to us. All we have to do is believe in Him and in His Word."

Ramesh was deep in his thoughts. He was trying to digest everything he had just heard. The question of eternal life, however, seemed confusing to him. It was not exactly what he had been taught by his parents or by the pundit at the "*shivala*" they frequented.

"Listen, Sweta," he said, "you say that, after you die one day, you'll live eternally in Heaven without any sickness, any suffering, any poverty, any death ... but, you mean, you won't reincarnate in another body?"

"Oh no, Ram. The dead don't reincarnate to come and live again on this earth. We are just pilgrims down here. Our eternal dwelling place is in Heaven with Jesus."

"But, Sweta, what happens to those who don't believe in Jesus?"

"Listen, Ram, I don't want to scare you. But, what I'm going to tell you is Jesus's own words. It's in the Bible. The Bible says: "***For***

*God so loved the world, that he gave his one and only Son, that whoever believes in him should not perish, but have eternal life.*"[17] As you can see, Jesus is a gift God has given to us. Through Him, we have eternal life. But, those who don't believe in Him, alas, will perish."

"Perish?" Ramesh asked, evidently frightened.

"They will be thrown into a place called the 'Lake of Fire'. It's a place where the fire burns throughout eternity and from where there's no way of escape, Ram."

Hearing that, the young man looked worried.

"Listen, Ram," Sweta comforted him, "I don't want you to think about the Lake of Fire. Consider rather God's love for us in giving us His only Son to die for us on the cross …Which father would do that?"

Reference to that Father-Son relationship resonated loudly with Ramesh. He couldn't

---

[17] John 3:16.

help thinking of his own father who had given his life for his family's survival.

"That sounds wonderful, Sweta. If such a thing as eternal life really exists, I'd like to have my share of it, Sweta."

"Listen, Ram. I can't tell you everything. There's much more than what I've told you so far. If that's okay with you, why not come to church with me this Sunday? You'll see and hear by yourself. You'll hear the Word of God and, I'm sure, that will do you much good. After the service, I can ask the pastor to have a word with you. The church members also will welcome you. You'll see how wonderful those people are."

Then, laughing, the young lady added: "And you'll hear me sing, too!"

"You?" Ram asked in astonishment. "You sing in church?"

"Yes, Ram. I am one of the praise and worship leaders. That is, I announce the song we are going to sing and the people follow as I lead. I'm sure you'll be touched by the singing – rather by the words."

"Everything you've told me, Sweta, is simply wonderful. I'd be curious to see and hear by myself. And, if it's to hear you sing, I think it's more than worth going," Ramesh said, stroking the young girl's dyed hair.

"The service starts at 10:00. Can you meet me at 8:45-9:00 at "Happy Shopping" supermarket in Curepipe so that we can get there by 9:50 at latest?"

"Okay, Sweta. I'll make it a point to be at "Happy Shopping" supermarket before 9:00."

"Good. You'll see how blessed you'll be, Ram."

Holding hands and laughing like two kids, the two left.

# CHAPTER 13

## SUNDAY SERVICE IN CHURCH

That Sunday, "Word of Truth Gospel Church" was packed full. There must have been almost two hundred people present.

Sweta walked Ramesh right to the third row of plastic chairs where Sweta's parents were already sitting. They turned to Ramesh, nodded and smiled.

The young man looked to left then to right, as if to reconnoiter the place. The first thing that surprised him was the absence of statues and images. The white walls were painted clean. At the far end of the room, was a podium where sat three gentlemen in their Sunday best. Heads bent, they, every now and then, lifted their hands and looked heavenward, their lips mumbling inaudibly.

"The gentleman in the middle," Sweta murmured in Ramesh's ear, "is Pastor Henri Duval. The two others are his assistants. They are praying and worshiping God."

The second thing that surprised Ram was the fact that the pastor did not wear any special garments. They were dressed in a suit just like so many other gentlemen present.

On the wall, in the background, there was just a painting with the words: **"I Am The Way, The Truth And The Life: John 14:6"**

On either side of the podium, a fan was turning at full speed. In the middle of the podium, in the forefront, stood a one-footed furniture with a glass surface. In the forefront were also three microphones on stands.

"Excuse me," Sweta murmured in Ramesh's ear, "I'll go to the podium for praise and worship. Feel at home. Mum and Dad are by your side. The two drew closer to Ramesh, smiling.

At 10:00 sharp, the pastor moved to the centre microphone. Smiling, he greeted the congregation and welcomed visitors and new comers. Already Ramesh was feeling at ease. He felt the love and the cordiality in that otherwise dull building.

The pastor then asked everybody to stand up and said: "Let's all raise our voices and praise the Lord."

Ramesh had never heard or seen something like that. All the people, eyes closed, began to pray audibly. It was loud, but melodious. It was like a big beehive buzzing. That collective praying and praising went on for about ten minutes. Then the pastor invited the praise and worship team to take over.

Ramesh sat up, stretched his neck, anxious to see Sweta sing. The band began to play. It was composed of three guitarists, a keyboardist, a drummer and a percussionist. Ramesh would never have thought there could be such a band in a church. At the Hindu temple, he was more used to seeing oriental instruments such as a harmonium, a sitar and tablas.

Another feature of the service that the young man found strange was the clapping. The whole congregation clapped during the singing to follow the beat and applauded at the end of each song.

Ramesh soon found himself clapping and applauding too – much to the satisfaction of Sweta's parents. Sweta's sweet and melodious voice was, to a great extent, responsible for that.

Ram liked especially *"This Is The Day That The Lord Has Made*[18]*"* and *"What A Friend We Have In Jesus"*[19]. The choir, then, sang a song in French and two songs in …Hindi! That was, indeed, a big surprise for him: Hindi songs sung in a Christian church! Two songs about the love of Jesus and about the beauty of Heaven! For him, seeing those women of Hindu origin and dressed in saris

[18] Christianity.com: Hymn based on Psalm 118:24. One version by Les Garrett and another y Isaac Watts.

[19] Hymnary.org: Words written by Joseph Medlicott Scriven (1855). Tune composed by Charles Crozat Converse.

singing about the love of Jesus – the God of the Christians – was astounding, mind boggling – surrealistic even!

After the singing, Sweta came back to her seat. Ramesh cast a glance in her direction to express his admiration. And the two exchanged a smile.

Then Pastor Duval stepped forward to the one-footed glass pulpit, placed his Bible on it and announced to the congregation the text from which he was going to preach. Those who had a Bible opened it. Those who didn't – or who couldn't read – just listened attentively. Sweta opened hers, drew close to Ramesh so that he could follow the reading. The text chosen was:

*"For God so loved the world, that he gave his one and only Son, that whoever believes in him should not perish, but have eternal life. For God didn't send his Son into the world to judge the world, but that the world should be saved through him. He who believes in him is not judged. He who doesn't believe has been judged already, because he*

*has not believed in the name of the one and only Son of God"* (John 3:16-18).

When the preacher began to elaborate on this text, Ramesh was amazed to learn that God, the Creator, was a living God, - a God of love, a God with human feelings and, above all, a good God who can give!

In Hinduism, he knew and worshiped a number of gods carved in stone, cement, paper and metals of all sorts - gods that have different shapes, several heads and hands. And, above all, gods that *do not give, but that demand* – even, *exact* - offerings and sacrifices!

But now, he was discovering a God who loves, who gives and who offers even His only Son for the sinner's salvation! Sons, in oriental cultures and religions, are precious – valuable. People would give anything to have a son. And here was a God who gave His only Son in sacrifice to man! What a discovery! What an eye-opener!

And, he got confirmation of what Sweta had told him: eternal life *is* a reality! It's possible to live eternally. Reincarnation was a mere fallacy!

While the preaching was going on, Ramesh, every now and then, heard the congregation say "Amen", "Praise God!", "Glory to God!", "Thank you, Jesus" and "Hallelujah!" in response to the pastor. He intended to question Sweta later on about "Amen" and "Hallelujah!" Those were two words he had never heard before.

As the preaching developed further, he learned that forgiveness of sins, salvation and eternal life are all free! Nothing to pay, no sacrifice to offer, no mortification to go through!

When the pastor explained how Jesus was betrayed and sold for thirty pieces of silver by Judas - a *"false friend"* – then arrested like a brigand, Ramesh's eyes filled with tears. Sweta saw him struggling to take out his handkerchief.

When Pastor Duval – a very convincing and eloquent preacher – mentioned how Jesus was beaten, spat upon, crowned with a crown of thorns, nailed to the cross and pierced by a Roman soldier's spear, it was too much! The young man burst into tears, sobbing loudly!

Drawing closer to him, Sweta squeezed his hand, trying to comfort him. She could feel his body shaking as he sobbed. The love of God had really penetrated his heart. The Holy Spirit had convicted him of realities he had never known existed nor even suspected!

After the sermon, the pastor sang *"Amazing Grace"*[20]. When he heard the words: *"**I once was lost but now I'm found; was blind but now I see**"*, Ramesh felt the song was speaking to him personally. He was discovering another God – a God who speaks to you directly.

When the Pastor invited the deacons to join him for the breaking of bread, Sweta murmured into his ear: "That's the Lord's

---

[20] Written by John Newton (1725-1807).

Supper I told you about. It's only for those who've been baptized."

Then, after a few seconds, she added with a discreet smile: "Soon, you'll be taking it, too."

And, turning to the young girl, Ramesh smiled, too.

After the Lord's Supper had been served, they sang a few more songs. Meanwhile, the collection baskets were passed from one person to another. Ramesh took out his purse and dropped in a few coins.

Then, a deacon made a few announcements after which he prayed a final prayer and wished the congregation a happy Sunday afternoon.

As people got up to leave, they shook hands, hugged or kissed on the cheeks. They all had a smile and a word of encouragement to share.

"Shall we go and have a word with the pastor?" Sweta asked Ramesh.

The young man acquiesced.

Sweta introduced the new comer and Pastor Duval welcomed him with a warm handshake and a cordial smile. She told the pastor how the young man had lately been severely affected by a number of problems and tragedies.

Having listened attentively, the pastor made him repeat a short prayer. Eyes closed and head bent, Ramesh repeated the words with all his heart.

*"Lord Jesus,"* he repeated after the pastor, *"forgive me for all my sins. I thank you for having died on the cross for me. Thank you for your blood that you shed to wash all my sins away. I welcome you into my heart and confess you as my only Saviour and my only Lord. Thank you, Jesus for making me a child of God."*

The pastor laid hands on him and prayed for him, asking the Holy Spirit to heal him of all the trauma he had been through and to comfort him. Finally, he invited Ramesh to the next service and to be a regular attendee so as to grow in the Word of God.

When Ramesh left the church building that Sunday, he felt extremely light. It was as if a yoke had been lifted off his neck.

Never had he seen the sun shine so bright nor the sky so blue.

The words resounded in his mind:

*"I once was lost but now I'm found; was blind but now I see."*

How grateful he was to Sweta for having witnessed to him about the love of God for us and for having introduced him to "Word of Truth Gospel Church". Through his encounter with the Word of God, he had discovered a completely new world with infinite scope.

Was Sweta not an angel sent by God to show him the way and lead him to Jesus?

On his way back home, that thought kept lingering in his mind.

# CHAPTER 14

## TWO LANDMARKS IN RAMESH'S LIFE

Three months after he first attended church, Ramesh was baptized in the sea at Green Bay. It was a glorious open air ceremony. About twenty people got baptized that day. As each candidate to baptism was immersed in the sea, the church members sang beautiful hymns, thus creating a really spiritual atmosphere.

Best of all, on 25th December of the same year – a date he will never forget along with that of his baptism – he and Sweta got married in "Word of Truth Gospel Church". It was a simple but glorious ceremony. All the church members were present to praise God and partake of their joy. Sweta's parents had invited all their closest relatives, but only two uncles and a few cousins came.

On Ramesh's side, even fewer relatives attended. Anyway, his family was not a very large one. Surprisingly, Gopal, his uncle came but left well before the ceremony ended. Ramesh suspected he had come at his wife Leela's request just to see how the Christian ceremony was held and, more importantly, to see what kind of girl that Sweta he was marrying was and report back to her. Two very good high school friends of Ramesh – Jean Michel and Vikash - were present.

But Ramesh didn't care at all for, as the Pastor had told him, he now had a new family – God's family.

Ramesh was dressed in a smart three-piece black suit and an impeccable white shirt at the collar of which sat a burgundy bowtie. With his well-trimmed jet black hair and sideburns, Sweta thought he would be a perfect fit to hold the main part in a Bollywood movie.

Sweta was even more beautiful that day in her immaculately white dress with a long train following. Her brow was adorned with a luxurious diadem. Her hairdo and her make-up were perfect. All the womenfolk at the ceremony had eyes but for her.

Ramesh had hired a cameraman to film the ceremony on video. Cameras didn't stop flashing. Never before had the young girl's parents been so proud. Every now and then, a little bitty tear would come to her mother's eye. But that was an expression of the joy inside.

On that occasion, Pastor Duval delivered a most beautiful message on a passage from the very first book of the Bible:

*"Therefore shall a man leave his father and his mother, and shall cleave unto his wife: and they shall be one flesh"*.[21]

When Ramesh heard these words, he realized how lucky he was in a sense: he no longer had a father and a mother to *leave* – which would

---

[21] Genesis 2:24, KJV.

have been very painful for him! But, he now *did* have a beautiful wife *to cleave to*.

When Pastor Duval said that Christ was the Bridegroom and the believers – that is, the Church – were His Bride, Ramesh realized what a turn his conversion to Christianity had been in his life! And, when Pastor Duval described the Marriage Supper of the Lamb[22], his joy soared heavenward!

The culmination of the ceremony occurred when Pastor Duval invited the witnesses to come forward for the newly-weds to exchange their vows. One of Sweta's uncles and a cousin stepped forward. As for Ramesh, a cousin and Jean Michel, his high school friend, stood as witnesses.

The pastor read the text of the marriage vow and each one, in turn, pronounced the traditional "I do". The congregation applauded thunderously each time. When the couple had exchanged rings, the pastor

---

[22] Revelation 19:9.

prayed for them and pronounced blessings over them.

Then came an unforgettable moment for both of them – the moment both had been expecting. Turning to the bridegroom, Pastor Duval said with a large smile:

"You may now kiss the bride."

And, when he did, the church building resounded with applause.

"Brothers and sisters, ladies and gentlemen," Pastor Duval said, "may I present to you …Mr. and Mrs. Ramesh Ramghuny!"

Loud applause exploded. A couple of appreciative whistlings were heard.

Ramesh couldn't help thinking of his late father and mother. How proud and happy they would have been to see their beloved son getting married!

They then signed the church marriage register, followed by the witnesses while the church choir burst out singing a wedding song.

When the formal ceremony was over, those willing to were invited to come forward and take pictures.

Finally, the church members and the guests came forward to congratulate the couple and give them presents. Most of them gave the couple an envelope with varying sums of money inside.

When everything was done, a keyboardist played a nuptial march and the couple slowly walked down the aisle, hand in hand and greeting with a smile people on the right and on the left rows of pews.

A modest reception was then held in a hall nearby. Soft drinks and snacks were served to those present.

When the time came for the couple to cut the wedding cake, Ramesh's high school friend, Vikash, delivered a very eloquent speech and proposed a toast in their honour.

The reception ended at 11:00 pm sharp.

# EPILOGUE

S tanding in the shade of the mango tree to protect himself from the scorching sun, Ramesh watched as the labourers he had hired worked hard to gather the crops.

"Hurry up!" he shouted to them, not with anger but to make himself heard. The "Sunny Beach Hotel" people will soon be here. We must get their supply ready. And there's a flight leaving tomorrow afternoon for Reunion Island. We must make sure the order is at the airport by noon tomorrow at latest."

Indeed, two years had passed since Ramesh and Sweta got married. Ramesh had contracted a new lease on the plot of land once leased to his father. He had established contact with several hotels and with other countries in the Indian Ocean. Reunion Island and the Seychelles had replied positively. Madagascar was still considering the demand.

As the demand for his vegetables had increased considerably, he had contracted a lease on another contiguous plot to increase his production capacity. To keep up with the demand, he had had to employ man labour. He had started off with five – three men and two women - and, now, he found himself employing twenty people – twelve men and eight women.

Additionally, he had established contact with the United Kingdom, France and Belgium and these countries have expressed their wish to import certain tropical fruits rather such as mangoes, litchis and pineapples. Ramesh has, therefore, begun to contact certain professionals to advise him as to how to realize that tempting project.

As for Sweta, she was still at the head of her uncle's travel Agency, *"Globe Trotter"*. Thanks to her job, she had a lot of contacts with foreign countries and with people from all over the world. She could, thus, use her contacts to do some market research and, hopefully, find some new openings for

Ramesh's business. Lately, she had talked to a German businessman about her husband's enterprise and the German had expressed his desire to meet Ramesh for an eventual business collaboration.

Not willing to go on living with his painful memories, Ramesh had sold the old family home. The couple had additionally contracted a loan with a bank to build their own house and buy a brand new family car. For his business, Ramesh had bought a second-hand pickup truck.

The couple has no children yet. It's too early for that. They have another plan before thinking of parenthood. For the end of the year season, they are planning to take a trip to Singapour and Dubai. This trip is long overdue: the priority for them is work. Once they are well established, they will plan for their first child. Thus their joy will be complete.

"Hello!"

Lifting his head, Ramesh saw his lovely wife coming. She threw herself into his arms, laughing like a little girl.

"How come you're not at the office today?" Ramesh asked.

"Well, uncle Kishore has given me this day off. He'll be at the Agency all day."

"That's kind of him, darling."

Looking Ramesh in the eyes and with a charming smile, Sweta asked: "After you're done with your day's work, can we go somewhere and eat something?"

"Of course, baby," Ramesh answered, hugging her.

"And afterwards, could we go to the movies? There's a very good Bollywood movie debuting at the Ritz Palace."

"Yes, Madam," Ramesh said, curtsying to her. "Your wish is my duty."

As the two laughed heartily, a swarm of colourful butterflies emerged from the mango tree and rose in the air, their wings fluttering.

Looking up and pointing a finger towards the tree, Sweta said: "Look, Ram, do you see what I see up there?"

Sweta's arm wrapped around Ram's shoulders, the pair, cheek to cheek, looked up the tree.

A little mango had just budded on a branch, cozily wrapped amidst green leaves.

# ABOUT THE AUTHOR

D r. Jean Norbert Augustin is a Mauritian citizen.

Since a very early age, he began to develop a great liking for writing. The fifty-two years he spent teaching mainly French and occasionally English at high school level further developed his love for languages.

In the seventies, he participated in a playwriting competition organized by the ORTF – the then French national radio – and came out among the twelve finalists over more than six thousand participants. He received a 200-franc prize on each occasion and his plays *"Entendu à Une Porte"*[23] and *"Le Syndicat des Gens Non-Nés"*[24] were

---

[23] "Heard at a Door".

[24] "The Union of the Unborn Children".

broadcast in sixteen French speaking countries.

As a Christian minister, he holds a Doctorate in Divinity and a Doctorate in Missionary Ministries. Consequently, he writes mainly Christian non-fictions. So far, he has published: *"Bought and Bonded by Blood"*, *"The Day Justice Was Judged"*, *"From Teacher to Preacher"*, *"Voices from the Cloud"*. *"In Quest of Truth"* and *Revelation Revisited"* – volumes 1 and 2.

*"Fatal Success"* is his first fiction to be published.

Milton Keynes UK
Ingram Content Group UK Ltd.
UKHW020246221123
432980UK00016B/946

9 798223 078586